TWO-DAMAGE MY HEART

TWO-DAMAGE MY HEART

C. N. HOLMBERG

PEGASUS

Book Cover Design by Melissa Williams Design
Interior Layout by Kristy S. Gilbert
Editing by Looseleaf Editorial & Production
Proofreading by Jennie Stevens

ISBN 978-1-7370164-2-7

To Whitney, Jessica, Alyssa, and Kingdoms.
May you never run out of adventures.

Table of Contents

Chapter 1

RUE

WHEN MY PARENTS asked me to clean out my old room, I thought I'd walk in to find my childhood in pristine condition, not an episode of *Hoarders*.

I supposed it was a little of both. My childhood—more so my uneasy adolescence—*was* still here, it was just pushed to the sides to make room for lots of boxes. Not moving boxes, mind you, which were slowly dominating every other room of the house, just boxes of stuff stored away until Mom could figure out what to do with them. The first cardboard treasure chest I peeked into had old grade-school homework assignments from Wyatt, my older brother. The second had a nostalgic bunch of old dishes I hadn't seen since before puberty, along with a buttload of mismatched silverware. After getting my daily exercise hauling half the boxes into the hallway so I'd have room to pack, I got to work.

Everything of actual use moved out with me roughly six years ago, when I finally decided to strike out on my own at twenty-one—in part because I didn't want my conservative parents and religious brother knowing I was taking advantage of my newly acquired drinking age, though booze turned out to be less fun (and way more expensive) than the TV shows promised. Shortly after that I met one of my best friends, Blaine, and moved into my current house with her, though she'd moved up to Washington to be with her sick mom a year and a half ago. Which was great, because I got to upgrade from the basement apartment to the main floor, but it also sucked because I loved Blaine, and the house was real quiet without her. A married couple rented the basement now, and I didn't really mingle with them. Newlyweds tended not to mingle with anyone but themselves. At least, that was the case with the newlyweds in Happy Valley, and I'd spent my entire life here, so I didn't really know anything different.

I turned slowly, taking in memories stirred by the anime posters and concert tickets pinned to the walls, ruining the yellow-painted drywall underneath. I'd painted my room yellow my senior year of high school because I thought it might help me with my depression. You know, since it's "happy" and stuff. It didn't help, but—surprise—pills and therapy did, once I was able to get my hands on them.

I'm good, now. But the cheerful yellow brought up sour memories. Pulling my eyes from it, I opened up a trash bag and started ripping memories off the walls. Not in an angry or even cleansing way. I just wasn't into *Sailor Moon* and *One Piece* anymore, and Aqua hadn't made new music for . . . decades.

I never played with Barbies, but I sure did like that song.

Once the walls were clean, revealing all the pin-sized holes I'd put into them, I taped up the bottom of my first box and moved to the closet. One look had me retrieving a

Sharpie and labeling the box GW for Goodwill, and many clothes I no longer fit into went into that, along with their hangers, because unpacking hangers is the literal worst. My parents were downsizing. Downsizing meant fewer hangers.

I chucked old shoes, pausing on a pair of red heels. I didn't own any red heels. I didn't wear heels much, because bunions, and everything fun in my life involved a lot of running or a lot of skating. But I started a new box of things to come to my house in Lehi, and those heels christened it.

"Oh yeah," I murmured as I pulled out a flail shoved behind my shoes. Yes, a flail. A spiked metal ball on a chain. I'd gotten it at the Renaissance faire when I was a teenager (possibly lied about being eighteen to make the purchase). I dug around a little more, finding a small dagger (complete with thigh strap) and a short sword with a pearl-studded handguard. I could never use these at Herospect, even as flavor for my costume, but maybe they'd look decent in a wall display. Heaven knew my walls were still painfully bare. I just didn't want to spend money on decorations, and so far all the cheap stuff I'd seen in discount store aisles didn't really speak to me.

The weapons went into my "keep" box.

I Goodwilled a bunch of belts, threw out some random trash, then stumbled across three shoeboxes full of letters. "Huh," I mumbled as I broke the Scotch-Tape seal with my nail and opened it. I thought I'd thrown all of these out.

An old birthday card, which had glittered all over everything else in the box, sat atop the mess. I opened it, reading through short and sweet messages from my family, before thumbing through the rest. Most of them were greeting cards, but there were a few old postcards from my once-upon-a-time pen pal in Japan, and my acceptance into the University of Utah. They were nice tokens, but not meaningful enough to keep in the long run. Setting the first box aside, I opened the second one.

Letters from North Carolina stared up at me, addressed in my brother's nearly illegible handwriting—not that mine was much better. I smiled as I picked up a few, then froze at the fourth in the stack, a shiver coursing up my arms and down my back, almost like the damn thing was enchanted.

The name on the return address read *Elder Harrison*.

I'd *definitely* thrown *these* out. Did I miss some, or just misremember?

Pinching the envelope in my hand and ignoring the *thump* beneath my ribs, I released a long, stale breath. Elder Harrison. Landry Harrison. He'd been my brother's roommate for a few months when Wyatt decided to join the LDS Church and serve a mission proselyting to strangers for two years. I was dedicated to writing Wyatt, and I guess Landry noticed, because he'd started writing to me.

His first letter arrived at the beginning of my renaissance, for lack of a better word. I was nineteen, finally out of the public school system, finally benefiting from interventions for my crippling depression. I could see the light at the end of the tunnel, and the timing of this letter from some random Mormon seemed fated. Having a sudden new friend, a new listener, and new letters to look forward to had honestly helped, despite his horrendous spelling. Landry Harrison had written me for a full year before going home to Florida and completely ghosting me.

But I was *not* going to dredge that up now. It was eight

years ago, I was over it, and this letter could burn in hell for all I cared.

I dropped the entire box into the awaiting trash bag. As if to stick it to me, that letter from Landry slipped out and stared up to me, calling out with my parents' address, and my name: *Samantha Thompson.*

Part of my renaissance had been changing my name. Samantha Ruth Thompson had been a sad, quiet girl who got picked on at school and struggled to get out of bed in the morning. My dad had always called me Rue, for my middle name, and when I went to college, I started introducing myself that way. I honestly often forgot what my legal first name was—I only needed it if I had to pay a bill over the phone or some such.

I chucked the other two boxes of old letters and the card on top, thoroughly burying any memory of Landry.

Dear Miss Samantha,

Greetings!

I know, your wandering who this letter is from. Hopefully Elder Thompson has mentioned me. He's defenitely mentioned you! So I thought I'd formally introduce myself. I'm Elder Harrison. Been out for 11 months and met your brother on my last transfer. I'm from Florida, so North Carolina is a bit of a change. It's freezing here! How's the whether fairing in Utah?

I just opened up with talking about the whether. I am so sorry.

Elder Thompson says you like to draw and play video games. What's your favorite game? I was really into Halo before I set out. You much for first-person shooters?

LANDRY

"And always, without fail"—I walked across the short stage, looking out into the small crowd of about forty people—"someone says, *sssshhhhhh!*"

A few chuckles sounded in the back.

"Every time. There will always be some librarian-raised person who absolutely cannot tolerate any sounds you, your mouth, your body, or your squeaky chair make." A few more quiet laughs bolstered my confidence. I paused, looking out into the audience, which I could barely see thanks to the bright stage lights. I adjusted my grip on the microphone. "And the shushing is *always* louder than the thing being shushed."

Someone clapped their agreement. I bit down on a smile.

"*Sssshhhh!*" I said again, holding the mic away so I wouldn't bust the speakers. "*Ssshhhh!*" I paused for dramatic effect. "I mean, I am offended when I'm shushed. Who here is not offended when they're shushed?"

More laughs pierced the darkness.

"And I just want to be *louder*, which of course starts the shushing war. *Sssshhh.* No, YOU *sssshhh!*"

I waited for laughter to die down before moving on.

"Who even decided that *that* was going to be our 'quiet' sound?" I asked rhetorically. "Why *sssssshhhhh?* Why not, say, *eeeeeeee.*" I imitated a mosquito. A few groans pierced through the ensuing laughter. "Or snaps?" I snapped my free hand. "Maybe we could just meow loudly."

I initiated my own conversation. "Hey, this movie is great! *Meow! Meow! Meeeeooooow!*"

The audience burst into laughter, and my canteen was

filled. I *loved* this feeling. Knowing the jokes I'd worked on for months landed. It was incredibly validating.

I raised a hand. "I'm Landry Harrison. Thank you!"

The audience applauded as I jogged to the stairs stage right and handed the mic to the stage manager before heading behind the curtains I was the last act of the night—just an amateur comedy night at a local bar, and my first gig since moving to Utah. I had no desire to pursue stand-up as a full-time career; I was in sales, I was good at sales, and I was comfortable in sales. And I was comfortable at small comedy venues with lax schedules. Comedy was a beloved hobby and a great outlet for me, especially considering I'd dropped myself into an entirely new world six months ago. I'd gone to school in Utah, but I was born and raised in Florida and made my name with Green Rabbit Solar in Florida. But when things fell apart in the Sunshine State and I was offered a promotion in Salt Lake City, I took it.

And right now, it felt really good.

I packed up my things while the stage manager thanked people for coming and recited tomorrow's lineup; I'd brought my laptop to get some work done and sift through my never-ending inbox. Ensuring I had my keys and my phone, I hefted the strap of my laptop case on my shoulder and headed out into the main room.

Small venues meant small audiences, so most of them were already out the door or headed that way. I started for a side entrance but heard a woman say, "It's not here," an edge of panic to her voice.

Glancing over, I saw two older women peering around the metal folding chairs, the shorter one digging through a large purple purse.

"Are you sure you brought it?" the taller one asked.

"I always bring it!"

"Do you need it?"

"I will eventually," she countered.

Curious, I stepped over to them. "Can I help you find something?"

They started. "Oh! You're the shushing guy," the taller woman said.

I smiled. "I am." I didn't mind the nickname at all—it meant I was memorable. It also meant that if I did this venue again, I'd have to come up with all-new jokes. But I liked a challenge.

The shorter woman said, "I can't find my inhaler. It's white and I don't know where it is." She clawed through the contents of her purse.

"White inhaler." I shifted my laptop behind my hip and started walking through the aisles, squinting because the lights were still fairly dim.

"Maybe it's in the car," the woman's friend offered.

"Maybe." She sounded unsure.

I turned down the third aisle, and my foot hit something, sending it skittering several feet ahead of me. L-shaped and plastic. I picked it up. "Found it!"

"Oh, bless you!" The woman with the purple purse came around and took it from my hands. "These things are so expensive. Bless you for taking the time to find it!"

The taller woman grinned. "Tell your wife she's a lucky lady."

I returned the smile, pushing against the tension in my cheeks. I was a fabulous actor when it came to cheerful facial expressions. I was in sales. "I'll do that. You ladies have a good night."

The shorter woman patted my arm before heading toward the door. I watched them go and, despite the front door being wide open, took the side door out to the street.

I was not married. Which was a natural fact of life, so I shook off the compliment. And that's what it was—a compliment. Not only was I a lucky win for an imaginary woman, but I appeared to be enough of a catch to presumably be married. In Florida, twenty-eight and single wasn't a big deal. In Utah, it literally made me a menace to society.

I rubbed my chest as I headed down 300 South, looking for my car among the slanted parking stalls lining the street. The sting wasn't their fault. They didn't know that, had the last year played out differently, I *would* have been going home to tell my wife how lucky she was. That hadn't been in my cards. But I'd had a great set, so I forced the pitying thoughts away and tried to focus on that final laugh, that final applause. It worked, sort of.

I arrived at my Tesla, my heart jumping when I saw a paper under the windshield wiper, thinking it was a ticket. I relaxed when I realized it was just a flyer. I tugged the quarter-piece of white paper free and glanced at it.

God must have a sense of humor, because the headline read *Singles Mixer at Salt Licks!*

Goodbye fuzzy performance feelings. Hello to staying up watching an action thriller so the only thing in my brain would be gun sounds and special effects.

Crumpling the paper in my hand, I tugged open the driver's side door.

"Landry!"

I looked up to see a few people coming down the sidewalk.

It took me a second to recognize them from church, and another second to pull up two of their names. "Angie! Beau! How are you?"

"Good!" Angie said. "We went to your show!"

A little bit of that validation—or hope for it—sprang into my chest. "Oh? How'd you like it?"

"You were the funniest one there!" the third person, a woman with auburn ringlets, said. I stared at her for half a second, searching her facial features for a clue—there. Mole under right eye. That was Martha. No, Marg.

"Thanks, Marg," I said, and she beamed. I was pretty good at names—I worked hard to be. Initially because it was drilled into me during training for summer sales in college, but later because it just felt good to know who people were, and it made people feel good to know you remembered them. Names were important.

"Yeah, you're funny," Beau agreed.

"Aaaand," Angie went on, "you should hang out with us tomorrow." She hefted an identical flyer to the one crumpled in my fist. "There's a mixer at Salt Licks. You should come!"

I pushed my practiced smile forward. "I don't know, guys. A single's mixer?"

"So you know about it!" Marg chirped.

"It's just an excuse to go out," Angie pressed. "And get to know people better. What's it going to hurt?"

She had a point, there. What *would* it hurt? I pulled out my phone to double-check my calendar, though I was already sure I didn't have plans tomorrow night. It must have been something about seeing the date in the grid, but I realized it was the one-year anniversary of . . .

Yeah, it would be better for me to be out socializing instead of home mulling over that again. I'd mulled over it enough to fill a cement mixer with cider.

"All right. Meet you there?"

Angie clapped. "Yeah, let's! Thanks, Landry!"

I waved as they continued down to their car. Marg called out, "Great set, again!"

I slipped into my car and reached for the buckle, noting again that I still had that flyer crumpled against my palm.

Sense of humor, indeed.

Elder Harrison—

Yes, Wyatt's mentioned you. I know all about the poop story and the guy chasing you off his lawn with a crepe pan. I figure that makes us halfway to best friends, no?

I'm including a printout of the 10-day forecast for Utah to put your mind at ease about the weather. If you'd like to subscribe to these printouts, it's $2/week.

Halo is all right. The story gets better later. To me, video games are all about story. Have you played any of the Final Fantasy games? Those are my absolute favorite, though I nearly threw my controller through the TV screen playing XII. Weirdly enough, XIII is my favorite, even though it's not as popular with the gaming crowd. I don't really know why. Something about the visuals, the depth of story, the characters . . . I just like everything about it. I like the escape.

Chapter 2

RUE

ANASTENE PARTED THE vines and peered down the dark, forested path ahead of her. She crouched. "I survey my surroundings."

Rhonda, Herospect's founder and dungeon master, flipped a page on her steampunk-designed clipboard. "You see a pressure plate ten feet away, straight ahead. You notice the sound of frogs and crickets has stopped entirely. The temperature on this side of the vines is twenty degrees colder."

"Cold enough for disadvantage?" Cameron, who wielded a foam hammer, asked from behind me.

"Not yet." Rhonda smiled knowingly over her round spectacles.

"I throw a stone," I—Anastene—mimicked the act, "at the pressure plate."

"How big is the stone?" Rhonda asked.

Anastene was a rogue, so her strength wasn't great. "A pound, give or take."

"The plate doesn't move."

"I do the same," Cameron said behind me, and also pretended to chuck a rock.

Rhonda lowered her clipboard. "The plate moves, and a dozen poison arrows fly out from the trees."

"Wait before going in," warned McKenzie from behind me.

We waited about ten seconds. Still crouched, I moved forward.

"You notice the ground under your feet feels different," Rhonda said. "Do you investigate?"

"Yes."

"You brush aside dirt to discover a granite plate about two feet long, one foot wide." Rhonda moved one hand to illustrate. "There's writing on it, but it's in Elvish."

I sighed. Anastene, a half-aquan rogue, which was basically a walking mermaid, couldn't read Elvish.

"Let me." Cameron—who was playing Drakon, a half-elf ranger—crouched next to me. "I read it."

Rhonda smiled. "It says, 'Here lies the bones of Corporal Hentwig. Let his remains be a warning for those who seek to follow.'"

Goose bumps ran up my skin. Corporal Hentwig was the guy we'd been tracking for weeks in-game, months out-of-game. And we just found his grave.

"And we'll take off from there next time!" Rhonda announced, losing the creepy Celtic accent she liked to take on when she was in character.

"Oh, come on!" complained Johnny, smacking his foam sword—constructed from a pool noodle—against the ground. "This is the good part!"

Adelaide, at the back of the party, stretched her back.

"We've been at it for four and a half hours. My sitter is going to lose it if we keep going."

Rhonda laughed. "I'm glad you like it. Next Saturday, same time. Also." She flipped through the papers on her clipboard. "Reminder that our end-of-summer bash is August twenty-ninth. I put a sign-up sheet on our Facebook group for food. *With categories* so we don't all bring sweet stuff, like last time."

"Boo," I called out, standing. "I dibs cupcakes."

Cameron grinned at me. "We could do medieval cupcake wars."

"No." Rolling her eyes, Rhonda stuck her clipboard under her arm and pulled the circlet from her head—it was fitting tight, judging by the marks it left behind. I had some jewelry pliers in my emergency costuming kit in my car—after we updated our gaming journals, I'd offer to adjust it.

Our NPCs—nonplaying characters—all immediately started shucking their costumes, which were really simple pieces we'd collected over the years, stuff from cheap Halloween stores, quickly sewn scraps, even burlap bags, depending on what Rhonda needed them to play. Sometimes they were monsters, sometimes they were townsfolk, sometimes they were sentient animals. Most often, they were played by Rhonda's nephew, Henry, and his friends, who were all still in high school. The three of them began chatting and passing around a bag of peanut M&M's.

I pulled off Anastene's arm bracers, which were made of real leather and took me *forever* to craft. Leather is the literal worst to sew. Make a mistake, and it's ruined. The bracers made it hard to drive, so they came off and the rest stayed on. I'd remove the other pieces—and my makeup—when I got home.

Sitting on a patch of clover in the park we used for our game, I pulled out my journal—essentially just notes so I could follow the story—and a pen. Cameron sat down next to me—he was a couple years my junior, stout, and good-humored. I was pretty sure he liked me, but he just wasn't my cup of tea, though I enjoyed role-playing with him. He started writing ferociously, since we'd had some big character reveals for Drakon today.

I tapped my pencil on my book and glanced around. Everyone had made it to today's session, including McKenzie, our healer, who I *had* dated for a few months four years ago, but we'd decided to just be friends. Johnny Lu was our wizard, and our married couple, Adelaide and Thom, were both fighters.

I'd discovered LARPing, or live-action role-playing, when I was a senior in high school. It's nerdy to most people, but it really gave me a leg to stand on. Started my renaissance, a scholar of Rue's life might say. I know it sounds stupid, but dressing up in costume, pretending to be someone brave and competent, helped me be those things in real life. It gave me the courage to stand up to my bullies until they left me alone. Gave me the confidence to stand up for myself, period. To get help, to get a job, to get a higher education. And it taught me to embrace my weirdness and make lasting friendships through said weirdness. In truth, when I was Anastene, surrounded by these other dorks in this park-turned-enchanted-forest, I was *happy*. Really and truly. Even more so than when I scored in roller derby.

"Two-damage," Cameron said, nudging me with his foam hammer. "Where are you, Rue?"

I rolled my eyes at him. Our character abilities and weapons all had different point values, so whenever we attacked someone in-game, we had to call out our damage. Can you say *two-damage* seven times fast without messing up? I can.

"Just thinking." I offered him a smile and jotted down a whole sentence in my journal before my phone started vibrating in my quilted satchel. Setting the book and pencil aside, I checked the screen.

Wyatt: I need a huuuuge favor please

I sighed and typed back.

Me: What now? I'm not cleaning out your room too.

Wyatt: Me and some of my buds are going to a singles mixer tonight.

Me: No

Wyatt: And I get a discount if I bring someone of the opposite sex.

Me: No

Wyatt: Come on, Rue! No one else can make it.

Me: Neither can I

> **Wyatt:** LIAR
> Dinner is on me

I paused, considering. Cameron glanced over and asked, "Who's that?"

Sighing, I said, "My brother," and Cameron visibly relaxed. Weirdo.

> **Me:** Minimum $25 value.

> **Wyatt:** $20

> **Me:** No

> **Wyatt:** Ugh fine. Pick you up quarter to six

Barf. I shoved my phone back into my satchel and tried to remember what I'd been about to write in my journal. Right, Corporal Hentwig.

My phone buzzed again. With a groan I ripped it out.

> **Wyatt:** Make that 5:30.

I checked the time. If I had to go people tonight, I should probably head back now. LARPing was sweaty, and it took serious scrubbing to cleanse the hand-drawn glitter scales from my forehead.

"Gotta go," I said, waving to Cameron and finding my feet. "See you next week!" I shouted to the others.

"Don't forget to sign up for the potluck!" Rhonda barked back.

But instead of responding, I checked Wyatt's message again. Singles mixer? This twenty-five-dollar dinner had better be worth every bite.

Note to self: bring a book.

Wyatt's friends were the kind of people you'd see on old TV shows like *The O.C.* or *Dawson's Creek*. Or maybe reality shows on cable channels no one had heard of. I-never-left-high-school-type people who all bleached their teeth and wore whatever the mannequins in the window of J.Crew told them to wear. They were nice, don't get me wrong, but something about them just felt . . . I don't know. Scripted, maybe.

We were all shoved into the back of some chick's enormous Lexus. I'd wedged myself in the back next to my brother, who was only eighteen months older than I was, so thankfully I wasn't emitting major baby-sister vibes.

"It's real!" the driver was saying around a piece of chewing gum. "I saw a video about it."

"Not everything you see on the internet is true," said a dude in the middle seat. I think his name was Terry. Maybe Jerry. Gary?

"You can't fall in love in thirty-six minutes," Wyatt said, speaking loudly to be heard in the front. He and I had the same (natural) hair color, strawberry blond, though mine was currently dyed a half-faded magenta. And while his hair grew in straight, mine grew in uneven curls, made all the curlier because I wore it in a bob. I didn't like it blocking the bedazzled name on my roller derby jersey: *Rue the Day.* And putting it up took effort, so.

Wyatt was a decent-looking guy, though. Hopefully that meant I wasn't too far behind.

"Not thirty-six *minutes*," the driver countered, stopping at a light. "Thirty-six *questions*. You ask thirty-six deep, meaningful questions to a complete stranger and really get to know them. Not just, like, favorite color and occupation and stuff."

"Question fourteen," said the gal in the passenger seat, "where do you hide the bodies?"

I snickered at that.

"Like, real questions!" the driver protested. "And then you stare into their eyes for like four minutes or something."

"Like a staring contest?" Terry/Jerry/Gary asked.

"No, you can blink." The light turned green and she drove forward slowly, looking for a spot to park. In downtown Salt Lake City on a Saturday night, that could get tricky. "It's like, I don't know, soul-staring or something."

"Soul-staring?" Wyatt laughed.

And that's why he didn't have a girlfriend. He could at least pretend to be interested. I wondered what it would be like to stare into a stranger's eyes for that long. Four minutes is short when you're busy, but to sit in a quiet room and just *stare* at someone . . . I couldn't even do that with Wyatt. Not for four minutes. Four minutes would be an eternity.

"Oh, right there!" The passenger pointed. "Go, before that other guy takes it!"

The Lexus made a sharp right, got honked at, and the driver cut the engine.

"Game time!" she shouted, and pulled a lipstick out of her purse, then used the mirror on the back of her sun visor to apply it.

I hadn't brought lipstick. Though I had put on some

eyeliner and mascara. I didn't particularly want to be here, but I didn't want to be the pathetic wet blanket drag-along either.

Hopefully this place had good food.

We piled out of the car, my seat choice making me the last to exit, and walked half a block to a flamboyant bar with a bright pink neon sign that read SALT LICKS. Admittedly, I liked the interior once I got carded and stepped inside. The walls were natural brick, the lighting steampunkish with Edison bulbs in every socket, and it had decorative brass piping every which way. I should mention the place to Rhonda, though she lived downtown and might already know it. The bar was small and in the back corner, as Utah bars tend to be. The opposite corner had a tiny stage and a screen that presently featured floating bubble hearts. My guess was Salt Licks had a designated karaoke night, which thankfully wasn't tonight. There were some couches shoved beside the stage to make room for four long tables to take up the rest of the floor, all lined with white tablecloths and sprinkled with silver confetti, like someone had been setting up for a birthday party and lost interest halfway through. Paper signs were stapled to the ends of the tables, one on the left with a male symbol and one on the right with a female symbol.

I checked to see if there were any signs for non-hetero pairings, but didn't find any. I wasn't surprised, but I shrugged it off. I knew a place a couple streets down that wouldn't have anything but, should they hold a singles mixer. Which they wouldn't.

I grabbed Wyatt's sleeve and pointed toward the bar. "Food."

He checked his watch. "Okay, okay, what do you want?"

"Tater tots."

He gave me a weird look and headed to the bar. Joke was on him—I looked up the place's menu beforehand and happened to know they served very popular buffalo tater tots.

Most of our entourage clustered to speak to one another, as did the several other entourages who had shown up for the event, yet seemed too wary to actually mingle until someone of authority blew a whistle or something. I should have showed up in a white coat. I wondered how far I could commandeer the event before someone stopped me or called the cops. I pressed my lips together to hide a smile, found a blank piece of brick wall, and leaned up against it to check my texts. One was from a group text with Herospect—McKenzie asking if anyone had seen her bejeweled contacts case where she kept her cat-eye contacts for the game. Another was from Blaine—the one who had shared a house with me before moving to Washington.

> **Blaine:** When are you playing next?

I pulled out my calendar to double-check before texting back.

> **Me:** Tuesday. I'll Marco Polo you some of the sweet action.

> **Blaine:** Lol. You should get a GoPro

> **Me:** Buy me one and I'll wear it.

She didn't text back right away, so I opened up a time-wasting bubble-popping game and played for about five minutes before Wyatt approached me, a plate of buffalo tater tots in one hand and loaded nachos in the other, a soft drink wedged between his elbow and side.

"Sweet!" I seized the tots. Popped one into my mouth. Perfectly crisp, perfectly spicy. I might have made a sound.

Wyatt snorted. "Yes, you're welcome."

"My thanks"—I popped two more into my mouth—"is showing up tonight, remember? How much was this?"

"Don't worry about it."

"I'm not worried about it." I poked him in the gut. "I get twenty-five dollars' worth of food. How much is left for dessert?"

He rolled his eyes. "Like five bucks."

"Ice cream it is." I scooped the nachos from his other hand and went to one of the tables. A few people were sitting down—I found a seat on a corner away from them and dug in. Wyatt kindly set my drink—a Dr Pepper, bless him—next to me before joining his lump of friends.

I'd nearly finished when the organizer—not in a white lab coat, unfortunately—got on the karaoke speaker and said, "All right, all right, we're starting in five! Please make sure you have a name sticker on and find a seat. This is a *mixer*, so don't just talk to your friends all night! Though if you brought a friend of the opposite sex for the discount, please let Marissa over there"— he pointed—"in the pink shirt, know."

I licked nacho cheese off my finger, gathered my food, and threw it away in the closest trash can, about ten feet from where Wyatt's group was conversing. I knew Wyatt was about to drag me over to get a name tag and a discount, but he could wait long enough for me to wash my hands. He called out as I turned for the bathroom, but it wasn't my name he shouted.

"Elder Harrison!" he called toward the bar, waving an arm. "Dude, is that you?"

That name scraped up my spine like a cold, rusted nail.
Elder Harrison.

Harrison is a common last name. This was the thought that whipped through my mind as I slowly turned. It was followed by the thought that half of the men over the age of eighteen in Utah have been called Elder. A tiny trickle of hope warred with fear as I, my joints suddenly tender as rotted wood, looked over my shoulder. At my brother approaching the farthest table and a guy in a blue polo laughing and waving and breaking off from his own friend cluster.

I'd written Landry Harrison for a year. Never met him in real life. But he'd sent me enough pictures—I'd stared and pined over enough pictures—to know his face, even eight years later.

That was him. That was *him.*

Nachos and tots warred in my stomach over which would climb up my esophagus first. My heart thudded hard against my chest, and my blood ran fast yet cold, surging everywhere but my face. That awful, cloying sensation of humiliation tickled my shoulders and stomach.

Someone pinched the timeline and cut out a chunk of it, I swear, because suddenly Wyatt and *Landry Harrison* were coming back toward the friend group, toward *me,* and my tongue was fat and rough in my mouth, like a beached shark or some other better metaphor that was not coming to me. I had no idea what to say to this guy. I was going to throw up. I was going to—I didn't know what, but I wasn't going to do it *here*.

I turned for the bathroom. *Walk,* I ordered myself. Running would draw attention. The last thing I wanted was for this ass nugget to think I gave two farts about him. I just needed to collect myself for a hot second. Make sure I didn't sit at his table. Claim I was sick—not far from the truth—and get a rideshare home. Pay Wyatt back for the food—

"Rue!" he called. Nope, didn't hear it.

"Rue!" he tried again, louder.

So much for not drawing attention to myself. I'd only managed to move six feet away from the trash can. Briefly wondered if I could just throw myself in there, hide out while licking clean my discarded nacho plate.

Plastering a tight smile on my face—I didn't do beaming grins on my best days—I turned around. Locked my eyes on Wyatt's face so I wouldn't have to look at the slightly shorter man beside him.

"And this is Rue," he said to Landry. Laughing, he added, "She's my 'date.' We do what we can."

Slowly, so slowly I could hear my eyeballs move in their sockets, I shifted my gaze to Landry. Square jaw, blue eyes, dark hair, and even darker eyelashes. Blue polo with the logo of a *gym* on it, of all things, and his arms said he frequented it. Designer jeans. Fancy shoes. The guy screamed successful car salesman. All while my insides twisted tighter and tighter, braiding to the point of bursting.

I wonder how that shirt would look with nacho barf all over it.

"Hi!" he said, low and friendly. He stepped forward and offered his hand. Like, to shake. What was this, a job interview?

My brain switched into social-cue mode. "H-Hi," I managed weakly, and shook his hand. Rather, I let him shake mine.

"Nice hair," he said, pulling back. He sounded . . . amused.

I glowered. "Thanks."

"It's crazy seeing you here!" He turned back to Wyatt. "You must be desperate to come to something like this."

Wyatt laughed. "Pot calling the kettle black."

"You're a year older than me, so it's less pathetic in my camp." He chuckled. Movie-star chuckled, where it was all in the chest and he flashed a full set of recently bleached teeth. He turned toward the friends. "Okay, let me see if I have this." He pointed to the Lexus driver. "Courtney," the passenger seat, "Mandy," the guy who sat in front of Wyatt, "Terry," and finally, "Adam"—he turned toward me and flashed a toothpaste-commercial grin— "and Rue, right?"

"Oh my gosh, I can't believe you remembered so many!" Courtney playfully smacked his arm.

I shrugged. "It's, like, five. And he knows two of us."

Landry chuckled again. "I don't count myself."

My eyes narrowed. *Don't count myself?* What did that even mean?

And then it clicked.

He knows two of us.

I don't count myself.

Two of us—Wyatt and Landry. Wyatt and himself.

Oh, my holy Batman, Landry *didn't know who I was.*

It hit me like a wave on a cold Oregon beach. Landry didn't recognize me. Landry *didn't recognize me.*

The organizer said something over his speaker, but I didn't hear it. My brain was spinning, tacking things together in a desperate attempt to make sense of the situation. Fortunately, thoughts are faster than words, so it happened just as the group broke up to take their seats at the tables.

We'd written for a year. Regularly. Like a-letter-every-week regularly. He'd asked me for photos and I'd sent them . . . but that was eight years ago. Seven, if you wanted to count from the very last letter. I probably looked different. I'd always carried a smidge of baby fat in my face until I moved out (stopped eating my mom's cooking) and joined roller derby. I used to straighten my hair too, and I wore it long. Now it was level with my earlobes, curly, and dyed pink. And I didn't go by Samantha anymore. Landry knew me as Samantha. I don't know if I ever told him my middle name, and even so, it was *Ruth*, not Rue. And Wyatt . . . he'd made a joke about me being his date, not mentioning I was his sister. He'd known I'd written to Landry, but he didn't know how seriously, did he? Maybe he just assumed Landry knew . . .

But he didn't. And it was both relieving and utterly infuriating. I knew *exactly* who this Sears-catalog ad for hemorrhoid cream was the second I heard his name. The second I saw his face. And he had no idea I was the woman who wrote to him, the woman who sent him holiday packages, the woman who had—*at the time*—maybe stupidly fallen for him. Even with Wyatt *right here* for reference.

That year of letters had been everything to me. *He* had been everything to me. But for him . . . was I so unimportant?

"Everyone needs to take their seat," the organizer said again over the speaker, and I realized nearly everyone had, and I was standing there like a doofus, staring off into space.

I should leave. But then I caught Wyatt's eye, and he gave

me a desperate look and tilted his head toward an open seat by . . . who was it, Courtney?

Biting the inside of my cheek, I stomped over, dragged the metal folding chair out, and sat down, folding my arms across my chest as I did, trying to act like they didn't shake ever so slightly, like I'd just finished a hundred push-ups. Trying to focus on anything else and failing miserably.

"The bell will ring every three minutes," the operator went on. "Then the men will stand and move down the row. There are arrows on the table indicating the direction!"

I glanced down the table to an arrow made of red painter's tape. Good, I wouldn't have to "date" my brother for three minutes. Gross.

But then I looked down the other way. I'd been so focused on getting out of the spotlight, on sitting down, that I hadn't realized *where* I'd sat down.

And in exactly nine minutes, I would be face-to-face with Landry Harrison.

Hey Samantha!

I was jazzed to get a response! Letters out here are werth their wait in gold. I'm not even allowed to email, though I know some missions allow it. Thank you for the whether bulletins. I would like to subscribe. Can I open a tab and pay you back when I get home? Just past my halfway mark, now. Burned a tie to celebrate (it's a missionary thing).

I haven't played Final Fantasy, but I've seen trailers and it looks amazing. Maybe you could show me when I get back. I'm going to BYU for school, so I'll be in your neck of the woods. I'm thinking about acounting, but I've also heard that program is really hard and time consuming, so . . . we'll see. Are you in school? What are you studying?

Sending a photo you will eather think is amazing or really dumb. There's a way to angle a camera at a crayon to make it look like you're holding a lightsaber . . .

Chapter 3

LANDRY

I'D MISSED UTAH.

I mean, nine times out of ten, I'd pick Florida (Utah gets a point because it doesn't have hurricanes). Beaches, amusement parks, suntans, Disney World, ridiculous newspaper headlines . . . Florida was a great place to be. But a small piece of my heart loved Utah, and not just because I'd gotten my undergraduate degree here. I loved the forests and the redrock and the skiing . . . which I supposed just summed up to "I like mountains." And the people were friendly and the pioneer history deep. Also, fry sauce.

So when Green Rabbit Solar offered me the position of regional director for the West six months ago, headquartered in Salt Lake City, I'd taken it. I had family in Florida, yes, but life was starting to get mundane, and a fresh start sounded incredibly appealing, especially after what happened with TaLeah. So I moved, settled in a new high-rise apartment and a new office, and breathed in the fresh air.

Now, sitting in Salt Licks and partaking in Utah's active

singles scene, it seemed God was on my side—running into Wyatt after so many years was great. He'd been my favorite mission companion, mostly because he always did the dishes and often let us sleep in. We were friends on Facebook, but other than that, I hadn't really kept in touch with him. I hoped to catch up once the event was over.

But for now, *ladies*.

The first gal I partnered with looked full-on cowgirl and spoke with a Southern accent, but when I asked where she was from, she said "Bountiful," which was a city north of Salt Lake.

"Oh?" I asked. "Your family ranchers? Farmers?"

"Oh no," she drawled, twisting one of two braided pigtails around her finger. "My dad's a venture capitalist."

I had a sneaking suspicion the accent was fake, which I honestly did not understand. What if we hit it off? What if I took her out tomorrow, and the next week, and the next week? What if the fates aligned and we got married? Would she keep the act up month after month, year after year?

I almost asked about her dialect, but the bell rang. Cowgirl jotted down her number and slid it to me with a wink; per the rules, I unseated and moved on to the next gal.

She was older than me, with loose brown curls and horn-rimmed glasses. She smiled faintly as I sat down.

"Hi, I'm Landry." I pulled out my best grin. "How are you?"

She proceeded to regale me with her recent divorce for the next three minutes. It wasn't necessarily awkward . . . I just felt bad for her. I had a napkin in my pocket from the nachos I'd indulged in earlier, so when she started tearing up, I handed it to her. She nodded appreciatively and blew her nose.

The bell rang, and I slid down next to one of Wyatt's friends—her hair covered her name tag. Blonde, C . . . C . . . Courtney.

"Hi, Courtney," I said.

"Landry." She grinned. "So what do you do and where have you been all my life?"

I chuckled. "I sell solar. Well, I oversee people who sell solar."

"Oh my gosh, solar is hot right now. I mean, I'm sure it gets *hot*, but you know what I mean." She smacked on a piece of gum, and I laughed good-humoredly at her joke. "Do you, like, go door-to-door?"

"Not anymore, but I used to."

"I hear some people make bank doing that."

I just waggled my eyebrows in response, which made her laugh. Visually, Courtney was *exactly* the type of girl I would have been all over in my early twenties. I really dug that chipper beach-babe thing—really friendly women who put forth the effort, you know? But while a nice gal like this would look picture-perfect on a Christmas card, I'd learned the long and hard way that the looks road didn't lead to lasting happiness. I'd spent so many years living in the *now*, chasing what seemed fun right at the moment, that it took me longer than most to figure out what I wanted in the *later.* I had five brothers, three older and two younger, and I was the only one not married. I had a good job—and yes, I was financially comfortable—but I didn't have anyone to share it with, and no prospects on the horizon. I'd hoped the transfer to Salt Lake would change that, but so far, no luck.

And yet, I knew that line of thinking still made me shallow. Courtney was gorgeous, but that didn't mean she wasn't also kind, smart, and deep. I inwardly chided myself. What would it hurt, taking a shot at Courtney? Speed dating was so short, so superficial. I wondered what Courtney was like within—what made her tick. What got her up in the morning. What motivated her to come to a bar on a Saturday evening and chat with strangers. Wyatt obviously liked her, if he kept her around. Admittedly, she reminded me of TaLeah, but I'd liked TaLeah, hadn't I? I didn't think I could screw up that badly twice . . . right?

"What do you do?" I asked, hating the requisite small-talk questions, wishing I could drill a little deeper. But these things took time.

"I'm an aesthetician," she said, suddenly serious. "I went to a lot of school for it, and I love what I do."

"I'd hope you do."

"Sorry," she offered, throwing up a hand boasting a perfect manicure. "Usually if I say 'I do hair' or 'I do nails,' people just automatically think I'm ditzy or, like, I took the easy way out, you know? But it's not *easy*. I had to do a lot of training. I still do a lot of training."

I nodded. "Absolutely. I have a sister-in-law who's an aesthetician. She's a hard worker for sure."

Courtney smiled. I could see relief flaking off her like dried paint. "Yeah, okay. That's awesome." She leaned forward. "I do a mean pedicure, and they're not just for girls."

I leaned forward as well. "My dear, I am no stranger to pedicures."

She laughed like I'd just revealed I was a Kardashian. "Okay, you're the best. Cancel your nail person and start coming to me. Here." She pulled off her name tag and scribbled the name of her salon and her phone number under it, and I wondered if she genuinely wanted me as a client, or if this was a sly way of giving me her phone number. I didn't mind either, to be honest. Not to sound like a prick, but God gave me a certain kind of face and a gym pass, and it generally wasn't hard for me to get women's phone numbers. It was just hard to seal the deal in the long run.

She handed the sticker to me, and the bell rang.

"Thanks, C." I stood. I'd learned in a sales training course that assigning people nicknames early on often helped endear them to you. I'd done it so much it just became a habit.

"See you and your feet soon." She waved.

I moved down a chair and sat, coming face-to-face with— Wyatt's friend, this time no name tag, period. I usually took one notable feature about a person and linked it to their name, to help me remember. Her feature was easy—pink hair. Pink, rouge, Rue.

"Hi, Rue," I said.

She sat leaned back in her chair, arms folded across her chest. She wasn't exactly glowering, but she wasn't smiling either. Almost like she didn't want to be here, or I was the last person she wanted to see. But I'd cracked tougher shells than this.

I flashed my best grin, but her countenance didn't change.

Instead, she sighed. "Let's get this over with. Unless you have some texts to check?"

"Texts?" I asked, glancing at my smart watch, wondering if she'd seen it light up. It simply flashed the time.

"I don't mind playing a game on my phone to pass the time," she said flatly.

I laughed. "Wow. Why are you here if you don't want play?"

Her mouth twitched like she wanted to say something and thought better of it, which piqued my curiosity. Rue was an interesting woman—nothing like Courtney, Instagram-ready and styled to a T. But she wasn't girl-next-door either. Pink hair aside, she wore her eyeliner like a modern-day Cleopatra. Her blouse appeared to be made of blue and white chevrons, but on closer inspection was actually patterned with cats. She had glitter-lined purple suspenders on. So not girl next door. More like a cashier at Hot Topic.

Her arms remained folded across her chest, and I noticed a nice line going down her forearms.

"You lift?"

"What?" she asked.

"Like at the gym."

She glanced at the logo on my shirt and rolled her eyes, which weirdly made me feel . . . small. Not something I was used to. "No, I don't *lift*. You have to be a really boring person if the only way you get exercise is going to a big building where a bunch of other people exercise."

I chuckled, not necessarily because it was funny, but because I wasn't sure how else to respond. "Okay, then what do you do? Rock climbing?"

"I skate."

"You skate," I repeated. "With your arms?"

She sighed like I was a child asking *why, why, why, why.* "I do roller derby. I'm a jammer."

I nodded. "And a jammer is . . ."

She frowned. "The person who scores."

"Is there like a baton involved? Or do you just shove a lot of people on the opposing team?" I grinned again, trying to lighten her up.

Didn't work. "Shoving is illegal. But I throw around a lot of swords."

I straightened. "Wait, what? Swords?"

"Yeah, you know." Now a smirk did catch her lips, and it made her look feline. And, weirdly, kind of hot. "Like the ones in Renaissance faires."

She said it like I should know what she was talking about, like she was quoting a popular movie or an internet meme. But I couldn't place it. And when I blinked at her, unsure, the smirk left. She seemed utterly exasperated with me, and I'd only known her two minutes.

The bell rang. Make that three minutes.

"Have fun selling solar," she quipped as I stood.

I paused. "How'd you know that?"

She raised an eyebrow at me, making me feel stupid. "You talk real loud, *Elder Harrison*."

Then she simply waved goodbye, leaving me wondering if I'd somehow lost my charm in the twelve inches between her chair and Courtney's.

RUE

"I don't want dessert anymore," I told my brother in the most pleading, hushed tone I could muster. Tonight had been an utter disaster. Landry aside, I was absolutely and completely wiped out from having to converse with strangers for a freaking *hour and a half*. I didn't understand how people like Wyatt and Courtney and Terry did stuff like this. I'd mentioned the weather at least thirty-five times to at least thirty people. I didn't want small talk. I didn't want to "share" about myself. I didn't want to date a single bloody person in this joint. I just wanted to go home and watch Netflix on my computer, huddled under a blanket, with all the doors and windows locked.

But Wyatt and his friends wanted to go out for dessert. And guess who they'd adopted into the squad? You guessed it: Landry effing Harrison.

"You said you wanted it earlier," Wyatt said.

"I changed my mind." The others were walking over, so I spoke quickly. "I don't feel that good."

"Heaven forbid you extrovert once in a while."

"*Wyatt.*" I smacked his arm. I should have driven here myself. Wyatt had picked me up and taken me to Courtney's, and she had chauffeured everyone else here. I was trapped. "There isn't even enough room for all of us."

"I can drive," Landry, who apparently had Superman's hearing, offered. "I don't mind."

The sound of his voice cut right through me. All those letters, all those words, and tonight was the first time I'd ever actually heard his voice. It sounded just as I'd imagined it sounding. All of it was just as I'd imagined as a stupid twenty-year-old. His mannerisms, his smile, his voice, just more grown-up. More moved on.

I wondered how he'd moved on so easily, while I cried into my pillow in the middle of the night, wondering what was wrong with me.

Taking a deep breath to steel myself, I said, "It's fine, I'll just get an Uber." I pulled out my phone.

In very big-brother style, Wyatt snatched my phone from my hands. "You're not calling an Uber. There's a gelato place right down the road. We can walk there." I tried to scold him through facial expression alone, but he was a dumb caveman and didn't read it. That, or he didn't care. Instead, he smiled demurely and said, toned exactly as the mother from *Better Off Dead*, "You *like* gelato."

I'll tell you where to shove your gelato, I thought, but Mandy, the gal from the passenger seat, was ushering us outside as Salt Licks employees began taking down chairs. I folded my arms, trying to make myself as invisible as possible, and dragged my feet along the sidewalk, keeping my brother between me and the others, grumbling in my throat and trying to think up excuses to leave that didn't involve summoning an emergency vehicle. Not that I could, since Wyatt still had my phone.

When we reached the gelato shop, I murmured, "Can I please have it back?"

Wyatt passed me my phone without comment, and I shoved it into my purse. Just a little longer. And then we'd be done. I was suddenly looking forward to the Lexus. Returning to the Lexus was the homestretch of this nightmare. And, regardless of my slights and my utter disenjoyment of what was happening, I was acting immature. Like someone had snapped their fingers and made me nineteen again. I was Rue freaking Thompson. I kicked skater and orc trash. I was twenty-seven years old and cataloged like the righteous library wench that I was. I could survive another hour with extroverts and a guy who couldn't even remember what an absolute jerk he was.

Probably for the better.

Determined, I marched right up to the counter and looked over flavors. There was a rainbow one I was tempted to try just because it was pretty and I kind of wanted to make a statement, but I also knew there was a ninety-percent chance it would taste like Froot Loops. So I ordered two scoops, one chocolate and one pistachio, then pointed back at Wyatt. "He's paying."

With a sigh, Wyatt came over and opened his wallet. I was the first served, so I glanced around to find a window seat or something, but the place was pretty crowded. There was one free booth, so I slid into it and dug into my gelato, eating slowly so I could savor the one good thing about being here.

Wyatt came up next and pulled up a free chair from a nearby table. Courtney slid in next to me and, to my disappointment, Landry took the opposite bench, sliding down to sit directly across from me.

I pulled my feet in and focused on gelato. When I glanced up again, Mandy had gotten a seat beside Landry, and Terry had also pulled up a chair, ensuring we thoroughly suffocated the table.

Mandy was chatting up Landry, asking about his job, which meant I got to hear the solar spiel all over again. What did I ever see in him? This guy dripped stereotypical salesman.

"Wyatt, what are you up to?" Landry asked when he was finished.

Wyatt shrugged. "Marketing. Nothing fancy."

"Marketing is what makes businesses successful," Landry countered.

"That it does," Wyatt agreed.

"What about you, Rue?" Mandy asked.

I'd been in the process of spooning gelato into my mouth, so I just shrugged.

Wyatt got a sly grin on his face. "Rue vanquishes evil and rules a kingdom in her free time."

I shot him a dirty look. Swallowed and pointed my spoon at him. "I don't rule a kingdom. If you're going to make fun, do it intelligently."

"Vanquishes evil?" Landry asked, eyebrow raised. His blue eyes focused on mine, making my insides squirm. In all his photos, those blue eyes had always shined, like they possessed a light all their own. "Are you a cop?"

"No." I stuck my spoon back into my cup. "I'm a cataloger."

"A what?" Courtney asked.

Landry pressed, "So you vanquish evil from . . . catalogs?"

"I vanquish evil from mislabeled Library of Congress files," I snapped.

Wyatt says, "Never mind, if you don't want to talk about it, don't talk about it."

"Talk about what?" Terry asked.

Everyone was staring at me now, Landry most of all—or maybe his look just felt more aggravating because it was him. I cast my brother a big *thanks, Wyatt* glare. I wasn't embarrassed about my hobbies, but most people didn't get it, and they put down what they didn't get.

"Fine. I LARP."

Mandy's nose squished up. "What's larp?"

"Live-action role-playing," I said.

Landry's face lit up with a laugh. "Wait, like those guys who hit each other with swords in the park?"

I looked at him and pasted on a fake smile. "Yeah, Landry. Those guys with swords in the park who know how to interact with people without selling to them."

"Ouch," Terry said.

Landry put up his hands. "I'm not selling anything."

I shrugged. And, quietly so not everyone would hear, said, "You sold yourself pretty well into this group, didn't you?"

Terry, not realizing he was speaking over me, said, "I had a roommate in college who played D&D. But the swords were all imaginary."

Landry's brows drew together, not in an angry way so much as in a confused way, making me feel like a Rubik's cube with one too many colors. I gave him another fake smile and finished off the rest of my gelato. Then, if only to give myself something to do, I shimmied past Courtney and went up to the counter, getting a scoop of rainbow on my own dime, keeping my back to the others while the employee dished it up.

I'd liked Landry, once. I'd *really* liked him. Past Samantha would have even, at one point, claimed she'd loved him, but that was because she was stupid and gullible and stupid. He'd been an outlet who listened to my struggles without judgment. He'd been kind and paid attention to me when so many others in my life were growing tired of my "antics," a.k.a. finding myself and dealing with sadness I couldn't control. He'd been funny and insightful, full of promises I didn't realize he'd never keep. He'd been so open in his letters, so sure of himself . . . and yeah, he was cute. Double emphasis on *was*.

But the giant dumpster fire of me and Landry aside, it was obvious to me now that his confidence was arrogance, his kindness was manipulation, and his attention was to reap the same: attention. He'd written to *me*. *He* had started this. And when it wasn't fun anymore, he'd ended it too.

I ate my gelato by the counter. Wyatt noticed, and after

another ten minutes his good-brother genes started to kick in, and he mentioned having early church in the morning and needing to head back. Courtney sighed in disappointment. Landry started a text exchange with her, and I didn't hide the rolling of my eyes at the affair. Not that anyone was looking my way.

When all was said and done, Landry went his own way, and we piled back into the Lexus and started the long, blessed drive home.

At least I could take comfort in knowing I would never have to see Landry Harrison again.

I've never been to a ren fair! I'm sure there's one in Florida, somewhere, but the Sunshine State doesn't exactly scream medeval, you know?

Are they really that great? We should go, when I go up to the Y! You can show me the ropes and introduce me to meed. (Mead? ha ha, just kidding. Mormon, here.) I'm not sure I have . . . what did they wear? Tights? Poofy pants? But I'm nothing if not flexible . . . Let's go. When is it?

Chapter 4

HERE'S THE STORY.

When my brother decided to go North Carolina to preach about Jesus for two years, I was devasted. I had no other siblings, and Wyatt was honestly my best friend. He advocated for me when my parents were hesitant, or when they wanted to straighten out their "not typical" daughter, or refused to let me get into therapy because of the stigma. Don't get me wrong—they're good parents. Just kind of dumb with the mental health stuff, like most in their generation.

But I digress.

I had just been figuring out my own crap when Wyatt left. And he had a dumb missionary rule that he couldn't email or call us on the phone, only letters. So I wrote him letters. I wrote him a lot of letters. I wrote anytime I was bummed out about something, or something exciting happened, or if I was just bored. In the beginning I sent him three to four letters a week, though after a few months I got a better grip on sanity and kept it to one, though I sent him packages about once a month as well.

Anyway, about a year later, I got a letter from North Carolina that wasn't from Wyatt. It was from Elder Harrison. I recognized the name because Wyatt had mentioned him a few times. Elder Harrison—Landry—introduced himself as Wyatt's mission companion, even including a photo of them together in their suits and ties to prove it. He said some nonsense about how I seemed fun and he'd like to write me, if that was okay. I thought it a little strange, but he seemed nice, so I responded.

Landry opened up to me immediately. He told me all about his family, about what was going on in North Carolina, about movies he wanted to see when he got back. He never tried to convert me to Jesus, which I appreciated, and, I'll admit, he was funny. Charming, even. His letters made me smile, and his openness helped me open up too. I realized how much I needed a confidant not tied to my friends and family, and not someone I paid once a week to talk to me in an office for an hour. Someone who had no preconceived notions about who I was or what motivated me. Someone I could just be . . . me . . . with. So I told him about school, about annoying roommates, and yes, even about my mental health struggles. He told me about his ADHD and how frustrating it was to forget stuff all the time, even medicated. And truthfully, I thought I'd found my kindred spirit. Landry just *got it*. He understood me, he didn't judge me, he made me laugh, and he was cute.

I wrote him as diligently as I did my brother. He always wrote me back, even when Wyatt couldn't find the time to. And, like I mentioned, I kind of fell in love with him.

Landry loved to talk about the future, the "when I get back." I'd mentioned a new movie, and he'd say, "That would be fun to watch when I get back," or, more often, "That would be fun for *us* to see when I get back." He hailed from Florida, but planned to go to Brigham Young University for school when the mission was over, which wasn't far from the University of Utah, where I was studying.

I've never been to Timpanogos Cave, he would say. *Can I get a private tour?*

Or *The Red Butte Gardens sound great! Let's go there when I get back. I'll pay.*

Not too long before his mission ended, after Wyatt had come home and gone to BYU himself, I told Landry about the UtahRenFest near Ogden, the biggest faire of its kind in the state. I'd discovered it in high school and went every year. I told him how fun it was, how everyone dressed in costume, how there were performers of all kinds and old-timey knickknacks to purchase and even seven kinds of root beers to try, since Mormons didn't drink. And he thought that all sounded like the bee's knees.

I've never been to a ren fair! Let's go. When is it?

I told him it was in May. He was getting home in April and planned to drive to Utah for BYU's spring and summer terms. We made plans. He'd meet me there, and I'd sew him a costume, because he wanted the full experience, but also because you got discounted tickets if you came dressed up.

Everyone always went to the faire as merchants, fortune-tellers, or noblemen, so I thought it'd be funny to go as peasants. I researched the costumes, aiming for something thirteenth century. Ransacked local thrift and fabric stores. Measured, cut, and sewed with precision. I was so eager to meet Landry in person it gave me insomnia, which worked out all right, because insomnia gave me more time to sew and study for finals. We solidified our plans in letters, and he sent me his email address, since his mailing address would be moot once he returned to Florida. I gave him mine, and my phone number too.

I made the best costumes. The faire didn't give out awards for costumes, but if they had, we would have won them. I even made a wimple and slippers for myself.

The day of Landry's return came. I was so distracted during finals, trying not to think of him being "free." Of hearing his voice on the phone for the first time. I knew he'd want to spend time with family, so I waited patiently. Took all my tests. Signed up for next semester's classes. Kept my phone ringer on loud, because I didn't want to miss his call.

He never called.

I knew he didn't have a phone—he'd mentioned needing to get a new one when he got home. So I shot him an email. I don't remember exactly what it said. Something like, *Hey, it's Samantha, enthusiasm this, enthusiasm that. Hope you got home safely. When are you coming to BYU? Blah blah blah.*

He didn't email back.

I double-checked his email in his letter, wondering if I read it wrong, but it was pretty straightforward and I hadn't awoken the mailer daemons. He was probably just overwhelmed, right? Going from two years under strict missionary rules to rushing to get to a school on the other side of the country. Seeing family and friends he hadn't seen in two years. Reintegrating into normal society. It took a lot out of a person. I'd seen it with Wyatt—it had taken him a couple weeks to get into a normal groove again.

A week before the faire, I emailed him again. Reiterated the plans we'd made in letters, said I looked forward to seeing him. Sent him a photo of his costume. We'd planned to meet there, but if he needed a ride, I could swing that. I reread several of his letters to make sure I had his timeline right, and yes, he'd be at BYU by now. He'd wanted to come up early to get a job. He was in Utah. He was just overwhelmed.

Landry didn't email me back. He didn't call. But I was young and twitterpated and stupid, and he'd made so many promises, sent me so many pictures, so I was *sure* it was all fine. We'd made plans. He'd been so excited about them. Excited about *me*.

So the first day of the faire, the day we'd set aside, I drove an hour north to Ogden in my peasant dress. I'd put his matching costume in a brown Harmons grocery bag and set it on the passenger seat. I arrived right when the faire opened. Pulled one of his photos from my pocket to make sure I would know his face, and I waited.

And waited.

And waited.

I was so twitterpated and stupid that I waited until the faire closed at 11:00 p.m. I waited *all damn day* for him.

Landry never showed. And I never heard from him again.

He'd ghosted me. Utterly and completely. No explanation, no apologies, no follow-ups. No phone calls, no emails, no letters, no postcards. Nothing.

I was heartbroken. Devastated. Landry hadn't been my boyfriend, but I felt like I'd been broken-up with in the most inconclusive of ways. And I was scared—so scared I'd lapse into a deep depression like I had before, that all the progress I'd made would unravel itself.

It didn't, thankfully. Yeah, it sucked, and I cried a lot, and I questioned everything, but I saw my therapist, did my exercises, took my pills. Threw myself into LARPing. Discovered roller derby. Pulled off eighteen-credit semesters and graduated early.

I had two shoeboxes crammed full of his letters, of his jokes and his promises. And I wondered how many other girls he'd coaxed into writing to him, just to . . . I don't know. Keep him entertained out in the field or something.

I'd burned those boxes. And I'd burned his costume too, never mind the hours and dollars I put into it. And I got over it. Took some time to come to terms with it, to stop wondering if it was all a weird mistake, to worry he'd somehow died on the plane ride home. But months later, out of curiosity, I'd looked him up on Facebook. He was alive and well and studying accounting at BYU.

I never asked Wyatt about him, and he never asked me—I don't think Landry told him how much he wrote me, and I didn't offer up the information either. I didn't need to spread the humiliation of being thrown away. But that's the story.

And Landry Harrison has blissfully forgotten all of it.

Cataloging was really easy, once you got the hang of it.

Getting the hang of it was the tricky part. You might think it sounds ridiculous to need a master's degree to be a librarian, but if you want to dig your hands into system administration, bibliographic records, and the mighty Library of Congress, you gotta have one. In the end, it's a lot of software no one has ever heard of and a million spreadsheets, but the atmosphere is quiet, the work straightforward, and sometimes hunting down information for an incomplete or incorrect record is kind of fun. Like a nerdy little treasure hunt. Plus, there's always something to read when I'm on break, so.

I glanced over at my supervisor, Patty, sitting in her office with a steaming helping of Cup Noodles. A big heart sticker on the spine of the book she was reading denoted it as romance. I swore the woman had read every raunchy romance novel known to man—at least the ones she could get in print. I smirked at her and turned back to my computer, logging in the last of the information on "Dairy Farms | Mechanical Farming | Smart Collars." Today I learned a *lot* about dairy farming, including that I would never in a million years be a dairy farmer. I would stop eating dairy before that happened. Not my cup of tea.

Also, cows were way bigger than they looked in the distance when you drove by a ranch. Way bigger, with hip bones that looked like knives. Those babies weren't messing around.

I submitted my information and closed a book titled *The New Millennium of Dairy Farming*, which I'd sifted through to essentially prove that the catalog entry was valid. I checked the time on the computer—almost time for a break. I liked to take my lunch break late because it made the day pass faster, but I hadn't taken my first fifteen-minute break yet. But first, time to take *New Millennium* back home.

Yawning, I leaned back in my swivel chair and reached my hands over head, stretching in the padded cubicle I'd covered with photos, my degrees, bobbleheads of characters from my favorite shows, and seven houseplants, including a Venus flytrap I liked to hand-feed anytime a spider or some such wriggled its way up to the third floor of Deseret Library Services. Then I swiped my book—plus the small stack of others I'd been collecting all week—and tucked them into the crook of my arm. Patty, seeing me leaving, called out my name. I knew exactly why, too, and wandered into her office.

"Would you take these down for me?" She smiled and handed me two thick books with heaving bosoms and Fabio wannabes on the front cover. Patty always had me return her romance novels for her. Sometimes I got looks from patrons, especially conservative moms passing by with their kids.

I stuck *New Millennium* on top of the novels, gave her a thumbs-up, and headed to the stairs. I always took the stairs. Considered it conditioning for my hobbies. And I liked Patty, even though I wasn't a big fan of the romance genre. Too flowery and unrealistic, in my opinion. And the metaphors. The metaphors were laughable.

I trekked down to the first floor. Agriculture was closest, so I moseyed over there, checking the numbers on the spine of *New Millennium* to make sure I returned it to the right place. You'd be surprised how much time our library clerks spent just walking up and down these aisles, squinting at spine numbers, making sure everything was in order. Because if one patron misshelved a book, it could be lost forever, even if it was sitting just a couple feet from its rightful place. When people checked the numbers and the number wasn't there, they moved on.

I felt weirdly bad for those books. So I always double-checked the shelf and the book's neighbors. Always made sure it was in the right place.

This one's home shelf was at eye level, and I slid it into place. I hopped over a couple shelves and returned two more titles, then ventured into juvenile fiction to return a book on bridges. Lastly, I crossed into the fiction section, down the row studded with red sticker hearts, and figured out where my supervisor's latest conquests belonged. One was on the top shelf, and I had to pull over one of the little stools to reach it. The second was on the bottom, forcing me to squat down to return it. I noticed its neighbors were out of order and took a few seconds to right them.

"I didn't know you liked romance."

I bolted to my feet so fast my head spun. Glanced to my left, then to my right, for the source of the voice, finding nothing and no one. But then a familiar chuckle sounded in front of me. Peering through the shelves, I saw none other than Landry Harrison looking back at me.

What in the actual ninth level of hell?

"What are you doing here?" I blurted, then remembered I was in the library and repeated, strained and hushed, "What are you doing here? Don't you live in Salt Lake?" Deseret Library Services was in Alpine, right on the other side of the jutting mountain that separated Salt Lake County from Utah County, a.k.a. Happy Valley.

He shrugged. "There's a new marketing book I wanted to check out, but the Salt Lake system doesn't have it, and Utah County doesn't do interlibrary loan."

My mind was running through all the terrible things I might have done to have karma bully me so thoroughly. I'd been five days Landry-free and it had been blissful. Now my pulse was erratic and my palms sweaty.

"Too bad," I said with a shrug, though in truth, as a patron, it was seriously annoying that every city in Utah County had its own independent library, meaning no one shared with anyone else. Behind the scenes, it was way easier for librarians not to track down and ship all those books, but I, too, have had to drive to another city just to scope out a book I wanted. Sometimes I still used McKenzie's library card number so I could just drive to Draper and get all the books. She had a Salt Lake County address.

I snatched the stool and walked back up the aisle, so of course the unwanted stray dog followed me. "How was it?"

"How was *what?*"

"Your romance novel."

I spun toward him when we reached the end of the aisle. When did he get so tall? He was not this tall on Saturday. He was all broad and loomy and stupid.

My chest hurt. I blamed heartburn from lunch, only to remember I hadn't eaten yet.

"They're not my books, they're my supervisor's." A dad with two kids walked past toward the juvenile section, and I forced the vitriol out of my tone for his sake. "She has me return them for her."

He cocked a disbelieving eyebrow. "She makes you drive all the way over here to return her romance novels?"

I fought against a scowl. "No, smart a—" I clipped the name as one of the clerks pushed a cart nearby, glancing my way. Taking a deep breath, I answered, "No. I work here."

He blinked. "Really? You're a librarian? I thought you were . . ." He motioned swinging a sword.

I rolled my eyes. Landry and I had stopped writing long before I ever went into library science, so even if he hadn't purged my existence from his brain, he wouldn't know this was my trade. "You don't get paid to LARP, genius. It's just for fun. And I'm a cataloger. I work on the third floor." Note to self: stop telling Landry anything of personal nature.

"Oh, *that's* what you meant by cataloger." He glanced around. "I didn't even know there was a second floor."

I waved my hands sarcastically, like a magician revealing his trick. "Ta-da. If you'll excuse me, I have to get back to work."

I turned and made it half a step before he said, "Actually, Rue, would you help me? I can't find this book, but the system says there's a copy here."

A chill ran up my arms and down my spine. "Ask Melinda."

"Who's Melinda?"

I spun around and pointed. "She's right—"

Melinda, the clerk who had been pushing the cart, was gone.

I took a deep breath. "Fine. But if it's a marketing book, you're not going to find it in *fiction*." I made sure to shove the appropriate amount of patronization into the comment. "What's the call number?"

"Uh . . ." He rubbed the back of his head. "It's called *Social Marketing Offline and On*."

I frowned. "So you looked it up in the system but didn't write down the call number."

He just smiled at me, as though being handsome would make up for his lack of common sense.

I turned on my heel and marched over to the nearest computer. Landry followed behind, his presence like the shadow of death. I wiggled the computer mouse to wake the screen and searched by title: *Social Marketing Offline and On*. It came up immediately, with a snappy blue cover and a call number leading to the second floor. I headed for the stairs.

"Are you going to write it down?" Landry asked, jogging to catch up.

"I have this incredible thing called 'working memory.'"

He chuckled. "You're funny."

That made me scuff a toe on the carpet. I glanced over at him. "Funny?"

"Yeah. I can appreciate a dry sense of humor."

I almost gaped at him, then remembered my mission and trudged up the stairs. Leave it to stereotype-salesman to confuse sarcastic loathing with dry humor. The sooner I got this book, the sooner Landry would leave, and *then* I would never have to see him again.

Please, karma. God. Allah. Anyone. Please let him fall out a window and into the back of a garbage truck. Please.

We reached the second floor. I started counting aisles. "Shouldn't you be at work?" I asked.

"I kinda make my own hours," Landry said with a shrug. "It's nice."

"I'm sure it is."

"You're a standard nine-to-five?"

I slunk down an aisle. "More or less."

"You like it?"

"I wouldn't have gone to school for six years if I didn't."

"Six years?" He paused. "You have a master's?"

I paused, scanning spines. "Master's in library science. It's a thing."

"Huh." He ran his hand back through his hair. "That's . . . cool."

"Real cool." I crouched and ran my fingers over titles until

I found the shiny blue one he wanted. Pulled it out—it was bigger and heavier than I expected, and I nearly dropped it. Landry lunged forward and caught it. I let go immediately.

"There." I paused. "You have to have an Alpine or Lehi address to check that out, you know."

"Oh yeah, I got one." He flashed another grin. I'd think nasty things about him borrowing a friend's card to get what he wanted, but I literally did the same thing, so.

"May a million fines be in your future." I saluted and stomped away. There were two stairwells that led to the third floor, and though the second was on the other side of the building, using it meant sparing myself from walking back with Landry.

He chuckled at my "joke" and called, "See you around, Rue! Thanks!"

Yeah, I thought as I ducked from his line of sight. *When pigs fly and I start reading romance novels.*

I made it upstairs, then ducked into the bathroom for my break. The bathroom had a little foyer in it with two couches, a fake corn plant, and a mirror, and then the tiled area with three stalls. I ensured the stalls were empty before I pulled out my phone and called Blaine. I still liked venting to people who weren't connected to the situation in any way. And people who I knew would take my side, regardless.

"Hello?"

"I'm moving to Washington."

"Are you really?" Blaine shrieked.

Now I felt bad. Flopping onto one of the couches, I said, "No, not really. Remember that guy I told you about, the one who ghosted me on his mission?" I hadn't shared the fine details of it—I hadn't told anyone. But Blaine had a lot of firsthand experience with being scorned by the male sex, so I'd commiserated with her in the past.

"Yeah, why?"

"He moved to Utah, and I just ran into him in the library."

She gasped appropriately. "Really? What did he say?"

"He doesn't remember who I am." I rubbed my eyes. "I'm just annoyed."

"Um, yeah. That's annoying." The speaker made a shuffling noise, like Blaine was moving the phone to her other ear. "Give me his address and I'll mail him a box of crickets."

I laughed, releasing the pressure building in my chest. "I kind of want to look it up now just for that."

"Speaking of addresses," she went on, "I'm mailing you a bridal shower invitation. I know, I know, it's a million miles away, but I miss you and the stenciling is awesome."

"Aw, thanks. I'm definitely making it to the wedding!" I couldn't get fitted for the bridesmaid dress, but I'd given the little shop in Spokane my measurements and was hoping for the best. Worst-case scenario, it would be too small and hard to walk in. Or too big and I'd have to pad myself with feminine napkins to fill it out.

I'd done it before.

"I'm really excited for you." I leaned forward. "How are your mom and Lysander?"

"Good and good. She's improving a lot. Might get off dialysis at the end of the year."

"That would be fantastic."

"Yeah! Fingers crossed."

I glanced out the window at the late-morning sun. "All right, I'm going to go walk some laps or something to get rid of this energy. Thanks for listening."

"No problem, Rue. And hey, you're amazing."

"Well, duh." I snorted.

"No, really," she pressed, tone serious. "Don't slough it off. You're amazing, and it doesn't matter what some doofus missionary thinks or doesn't think. Remember that."

My heart warmed at the sentiment, then cooled. *And that's why I'm still single, right? Because I'm so amazing?* In truth, I didn't mind being single. I liked keeping my own schedule and doing whatever I wanted, whenever I wanted. I liked freedom. But sometimes it was nice having someone perpetually in your corner. You know, like *that*. Sometimes it was nice to have someone to make out with. And do other things with. And admittedly, it'd been a while.

Bleh. I needed to walk.

"Okay," I said. "Love you."

"Love you, nerd."

And I hung up.

I actually have felt phenomenal all month. I think this might be my new normal, though I'm scared to hope it is, you know? Hoping for things makes it hurt more if and when it all crumbles. But I really want to hope. And even if it all falls apart and I have to start from square one, the least I could do is enjoy the high while I'm on it, right?

But enough about that. I don't want to bore you. That sucks about your ADHD. I didn't realize it worked like that. Everyone always talks about it so jokingly, you know? Like that joke, how many kids with ADHD does it take to screw in a lightbulb? (How many?) Let's go ride bikes! But in truth, it's hard. And I didn't know there were different levels of it either. But you seem to be doing great! And I hope you do great. I always thought that the best way to get back at naysayers and bullies was to be successful. So keep at it, Elder Harrison. I believe in you.

Chapter 5

AT LEAST THERE'S always LARPing.

Whatever it's been the last ten years—failed midterm, broken heart, low self-esteem, family drama, lost jobs—I always had LARPing.

Herospect was my safe space. A place where I could be surrounded by like-minded people with no judgment, a place where I could create my own role model, a place where I could speak my mind and let my energy out into the universe. Unlike roller derby, LARP had no scorekeeping and no spectators. Just a few simple rules and fun.

So on Saturday I threw myself into the game. It was easy, because Rhonda laid out a master labyrinth for us to traverse by tying different-colored yarn around trees, and my character Anastene's rogue abilities came into play again and again. It's always bolstering to feel useful to the party. And we ended up fighting a horde of goblins. I swung my foam sword enough times that I'd be sore tomorrow, and it felt good.

I poured bottled water over my hair and neck when we were done, shaking out heat and sweat, then stretched until I was sure I'd at least be functional come morning. I plopped between Cameron and Adelaide to write in my journal, but there wasn't much to say when half the session was a battle. *Fought goblins. Raided bodies. Collected 236 copper. Tomorrow* (by which I meant next week) *we try to solve the riddle and open the iron door.*

"You were on fire today," Cameron said as I put the notebook away. He nudged me with his elbow. "Man, I should play a rogue next campaign."

I smiled. "But you'd have to actually be quiet."

He elbowed me again. "*In-game* I would be."

I smirked. "Nah, it's fun. I really like it. I kind of want to play a shapeshifter sometime, but . . . I don't know. I feel like I'd have to change costumes every time to really get into it, and no one has time for that."

"Or money." He rolled his eyes. "Seriously, faux leather is breaking my bank."

I laughed. "Listen. We'll drive out to Nephi for some old-fashioned cow tipping, then harvest some *real* leather for your costume."

"Oh, gross." He laughed. "The scariest thing is that you totally would."

Adelaide, one of our fighters, said, "Even Rue wouldn't randomly murder some guy's cow."

"But," her husband, Thom, chipped in, "if we do this, we'll need a large cooler. Free steak!"

I chuckled. "I wonder how much steak we could carve out before we got caught."

"This isn't Minecraft," Cameron added.

But Thom looked dreamily into the distance and said, "Free steak . . ."

Cameron nudged me again. "Want a ride home?"

I flicked him in the shoulder. "I drove here."

"Oh, right."

Cameron habitually and conveniently forgot that I owned both a vehicle and a driver's license. He'd offered to carpool before, but he lived north of our park, and I lived south. I guess maybe it was cute, when I was in a good mood.

Meh.

I stood and offered Cameron a hand, helping him to his feet.

"Reminder—" Rhonda began.

"That the potluck is August twenty-ninth," McKenzie and I said in unison, then exchanged a knowing glance.

Rhonda merely put fists on her hips. "Great. If you know when it is, then *why haven't you signed up for the potluck?*"

Whoops. "I'll do it right now." I pulled out my phone.

"There will be a raffle for characters to earn new loot," Rhonda went on, reading down her clipboard. "And a preview for the next campaign."

"Already?" Adelaide asked.

Rhonda nodded. "We've been at this one for eighteen months! And Joseph wants to come back, but not at the end of a campaign. I have some ideas." Her eyes took on a mischievous glint.

"Guess I'll be figuring out that next character." We'd probably have another few months on this campaign. It would suck to say goodbye to Anastene, but it was always fun coming up with a new persona to play, with new abilities, new goals, and a new history. Kind of like finishing an amazing book series, only to start a better one.

Which meant I got to design a new costume. Sweet. Me and my dress form hadn't been on a date for a while.

Turning around, I scanned the grass for my purse, only to find it not there. I paused, checking my person, then scanning a wider radius. I didn't leave it in the car—I'd been fishing in it for gum just a few minutes ago.

"Hey, Kenz"—I glanced at McKenzie—"have you seen my bag?"

She blinked and glanced around. "I saw it a second ago . . ."

Frowning, I started toward Thom, only to hear jogging behind me. Cameron, pink-cheeked, came up, my purse clutched in his hand. He was coming from the parking lot. I hadn't even noticed him leave.

I was about to thank him when he said, "I started your car for you so the AC would be on." He beamed.

The skin on my back prickled. But the guy seemed so damned pleased with himself, it felt cruel to tell him it was creepy to steal someone's purse and access their car without their knowledge. My mind quickly scrolled through the contents of my bag. The worst thing in there was a tampon.

"Uh, thanks." My enthusiasm was lacking, but he didn't seem to notice. I took my bag back. Quickly peeked inside, but my wallet and everything was in there—not that Cameron would rob me. Shaking it off, I turned to the others and waved. "See you guys on Facebook."

By the time I got to my still-hot car, everything felt more or less right again.

The following Friday, Wyatt turned twenty-nine.

I'd sent him the obligatory happy birthday text with five million emoji, plus a GIF of flexing, shirtless firemen just because I knew he'd hate it. Wyatt was picky AF—one of his worst qualities was returning about three-quarters of all gifts he received—whether birthday, Christmas, or anything in between—in order to get something he wanted more. (Which wasn't nearly as bad as my father, who would literally just buy his own gifts and then have us pay him back for them.)

So I'd gotten him a gift card to Scheels, wrapped it in plastic wrap, frozen that in a giant block of ice, wrapped *that* in plastic wrap, then put it in an oversize box filled with packing peanuts because what else are sisters good for?

While my brother's gift sat in the chest freezer I'd inherited from Blaine, I decided to do myself up. No one really saw me at the library. Anastene's look took effort, but it was bizarre, not beautiful. I didn't do my hair or wear makeup for derby games or practice because my head was always in a helmet, and I'd just sweat off anything else. So when I got home from work and had a few minutes, I decided to doll up a little, just to remind myself that I could.

I wasn't big on foundation, but I did use concealer and loose powder. I was wearing a fun red-sequin blouse to the event, so I went bold with gold and red eyeshadow, completing it with a liquid eyeliner wing tip in the blackest black Target carried. Two layers of mascara, some eyebrow touch-up, natural-looking blush and highlighter. I always felt weird if I wore both bold eyeshadow and bold lipstick, so I found a fancy vegan lip gloss that smelled like watermelon and smeared that on. Got my hair wet and actually put product on it. Diffused it like a pro, which was way easier with it short. (When it was long, it took me a solid hour to make it look nice. Curls are evil.) When all was said and done, I thought I looked pretty good. Good enough to turn heads if I showed up at a Magic: The Gathering tournament, for sure.

I pulled out Wyatt's gift, stuck a bow on it, and lugged it out to my car, then started the drive to Salt Lake City.

Usually, birthdays weren't that big of a deal in my family, but my mother wanted to have a big bash for Wyatt's twenty-ninth. She was one of those crazies who subscribed to worth by age, and since thirty was apparently the end of the world in her book, she wanted to make a big deal of Wyatt being twenty-nine, his last year as, I don't know, an eligible bachelor or worthwhile human being or something. I think she was just mad that he wasn't married yet and wanted a reason to bring a lot of single women to a party. That woman coveted grandkids the way Mormons coveted Jell-O.

(Utah thing.)

Thanks to traffic, I got there about fifteen minutes late. I parked by the grass, checked my fancy face in the mirror, and slipped out of the car, winding around to the trunk to heft out my gift.

I heard a familiar voice ask, "Rue?"

Wrapped ice block in hand, I turned to see none other than Cameron Chussey standing on the curb between parking lot and park, working a Frisbee in his hands.

"Cameron?" I blinked a couple times. Cameron didn't know Wyatt, so I was surprised to see him. "What are you doing here?"

"Oh, just throwing a disk around." He spun the Frisbee on his index finger.

I peered behind him. Outside the pavilion, I only saw a mom and her two young kids. "Is that your sister or something?"

He looked confused, then glanced over his shoulder. "Oh, yeah. She's in town."

"Staying with you?"

"Yeah."

"Don't you live in Orem?" Orem was at the southern end of Utah Valley. I lived in Lehi, which was at the northern end. Wyatt's party was in Midvale, which was a twenty-minute drive north from Lehi in good traffic. From Provo, it was forty-five, minimum. Pretty out of the way, especially considering how many parks were between here and Orem.

"Oh, yeah, but we wanted to come here." He gestured to the small park.

"Right." I nodded. My hands were getting cold. "I'm due over there"—I tipped my head toward the pavilion—"and I'm late, but nice seeing you. Have fun with your sister."

He smiled. "Yeah, thanks, Rue."

Hefting my gift, I closed my trunk with my elbow and crossed the lawn to the party. Mom had taped looping lines of crepe paper around the pavilion, and there were little clusters of silver and orange balloons on a smattering of circular tables covered in disposable peach tablecloths. She'd gotten a local Mexican place to cater, and they'd set up on the north side of the pavilion, their silver trays matching the color scheme, and I wondered if Mom did that on purpose. A handful of people were in line, several at tables—I noted aunts, uncles, and niblings—and another couple handfuls standing around.

Spying the gift table, I trekked there first, my two-inch heels (that was the absolute highest I could tolerate) clacking on cement as I went. I dropped it off, pleased to see it was the biggest one there, then turned and searched for Wyatt. I caught Courtney's eye, and she waved enthusiastically at me. Couldn't help but wave back. She was pretty nice. Behind her was Wyatt, his back to me.

To jump on him or not to jump on him, that was the question. I *had* donned pants, so . . . it was a possibility.

Stepping with a lighter foot, I approached from behind, deciding last second to grab my brother's sides. Sure enough, he jumped, then spun around and nearly elbowed me in the face.

"Happy birthday!" I laughed and dodged as he tried to get me in a headlock, reminiscent of childhood noogies.

"I got you a present!" I blurted as I dodged his big man-hands a second time.

He paused. "Is it a big present?"

"Technically."

His ginger eyebrows lowered, and he glanced toward the gift table. "All right. You're off the hook. *For now.*"

I snorted and punched him lightly in the ribs. "You should probably open it first."

"Why?"

Because it'll melt. I just shrugged, which was response enough as far as Wyatt was concerned.

"Rue, that is the cutest shirt," Courtney jutted in, stirring a straw around in what looked like a dirty soda. Was there a soda bar here? "Where did you get it?"

"Um." I glanced down, trying to remember. "I think a thrift shop in St. George? But thanks."

"Ah. Cute." She took a sip.

And that's when I saw him from the corner of my eye. I'd been so focused on Wyatt and avoiding his knuckles grinding into my scalp I hadn't noticed who he was talking to.

Landry Harrison.

My heart peeled like a Thanksgiving potato. Were they *friends* now? Was there no peace in the world?

"Yeah, it's cute," Landry said, holding his own soda, and my stomach clenched as his eyes dropped down to my toes and worked their way back up, making me itch beneath my skin. "You look really nice, Rue."

If it were any other hot guy telling me I looked pretty, I might have preened a little. It wasn't exactly a common occurrence for me. Or, were this, say, seven years ago, I would have flushed like a virgin bride and beamed like the sun.

But now it just stirred up all that settled dust, dirt, and debris that I had to hose down after every single run-in I had with this guy. And after every instance, I told myself it was the last time. Why was it still not the last time?

Why did my chest still hurt every time I saw him?

I had no choice. I had to disown Wyatt. Lord help me, I had to disown Wyatt and move to . . . where did people *not* buy solar? Maine? Was it really cloudy in Maine?

Fortunately, while my thoughts were running rampant, auto-Rue kicked in and offered a half-hearted, "Thanks."

And I wondered how bad of a sister I would be if I left the party early.

LANDRY

Admittedly, I was kind of hoping Rue would show up to this event. A lot of Wyatt's family was here—he introduced me to his parents, who were super nice—and a few of the friends from the singles mixer a month ago, but Rue hadn't been among them. I'd arrived early, a stickler for punctuality, and glanced over the pavilion from time to time or subtly scanned the parking lot. I didn't want to ask after her unless I needed to. I had the trump card of returning that book to the library in my back pocket, if I needed it.

Because I kind of liked her.

Rue seemed like someone who generally did not give two anythings about what others thought about her. She had her own drum and she was happy beating it, and honestly, working with salespeople—many of which wore facades and said yes to anything and everything I asked—day after day, I found it refreshing. Rue had a crackling-dry sense of humor and wasn't afraid to speak her mind, as I'd quickly learned after teasing her about LARPing. She seemed sure of herself without any help from the people around her, and she was snarky in a not-pick-me-girl way. In truth, she was the exact opposite of TaLeah in every conceivable way, even in looks.

But . . . she was kinda hot. Like, nerdy hot. And right now, seeing her dolled up, popped with bright colors and curve-hugging jeans, natural curls unnaturally pink and bouncing around her jaw . . . I felt like I was in some sort of video game, and she was the heroine barking at me to suit up, grab my gun, and go fight the bad guys.

I hadn't played a video game for a while, but I would definitely pick up this one. She seemed pretty close to Wyatt, but they definitely weren't dating, especially if they'd both gone to the singles mixer.

So maybe I had a shot.

"You want a drink or anything?" I offered, gesturing to the unmanned soda station at the end of the buffet.

She chewed on the inside of her lightly glossed lip. "You know what, I'll just get my food now. You two chat." She nudged Wyatt closer and ducked behind him, taking a roundabout way to the food. I watched her go, legs strutting like she was in a hurry . . . and like she had some good musculature underneath.

Hadn't someone said something about roller derby? I wondered when the next game was.

"Oh, Mandy's here." Courtney waved her arm to catch the eye of Mandy, another gal who had been at the mixer.

"How do you guys know each other?" I asked.

Wyatt answered, "Courtney and Mandy are both in my ward."

"And live in the same complex," Courtney said with a pleasing grin. "He fixes our broken things and we make him pizza."

"Mmm, homemade pizza," I said, glancing toward the caterers. Rue was spooning beans onto her plate.

Wyatt's mom appeared between us, and she grasped Wyatt's forearm. "Wy, you should go get something to eat before it gets cold!"

Wyatt laughed. "They have burners under everything."

"Well, you should eat before the yellow jackets get everything." She swatted as though one was buzzing around her. Her warm eyes fell to me. "Landry, have you eaten? You look like you need to eat."

I laughed. "I do?"

"Get over there, guys. I have a lot planned!" She clapped her hands, nodded to Courtney, then headed toward the gifts, pausing to greet Mandy.

"Food it is," I said. "Thanks for inviting me, man."

"Of course! Besides, more gifts for me."

Chuckling, I headed for the buffet.

Rue had already sat down, choosing a table full of Wyatt's relatives that had no vacant seats.

Mrs. Thompson threw a pretty good birthday party.

The food was good, the company lively. There were bingo cards at every seat, each square containing something about Wyatt: his favorite color (green), his favorite video game (*Mass Effect*), his occupation (marketing), and so on. We played three rounds, and I won the second. Mrs. Thompson wan't stingy on the prizes either—I got a panini press and a loaf of artisan bread.

Apparently there was supposed to be karaoke, but Wyatt had begged them to skip it, so we went right into a video Wyatt's dad had put together. Setting up the screens required shuffling chairs; the two closest tables were folded up, including the one Rue sat at, forcing her to sit elsewhere. Courtney waved her over, and she ended up sitting right in front of me. I leaned forward and asked her what she got her brother, to which she responded, "A puddle."

I wondered at that while we watched a five-minute video of Wyatt growing up, a lot of the women awing at his childhood pictures, and many of us laughing at the video clips. A couple family photos showed his sister, who looked like his twin. An uncomfortable niggling squelched in my gut, but I ignored it. Samantha was a long time ago, and she wasn't here, besides. I hadn't asked after her, but I figured she'd moved out of state for work, probably married with kids.

"Hey, that's me!" I said when a mission photo came up, Wyatt and me in black suits and black name tags standing by the Neuse River. I was in one other one too, but that was it—Wyatt and I had been companions and roommates for only six weeks.

When the video ended, we shuffled again, this time crowding around the gift table like we were kids again, watching Wyatt open his presents. He went for a large one first, an unwrapped box with only a bow stuck on the top of it. And it was . . . dripping.

I glanced at Rue, who met my eye, then quickly looked away.

"What the actual . . ." Wyatt laughed as he peeled apart soggy cardboard and lifted a half-melted block of ice out of packing peanuts. There was a gift card frozen at the center of it. "What is wrong with you?" he asked good-naturedly.

"You have to work for the money." Rue smiled. She was really pretty when she smiled. I checked my watch. This shindig would be ending soon—I could probably catch her before she headed out. Her weekend was probably already booked, but—I checked my phone calendar—I could make next weekend work.

Wyatt hefted the ice and threw it on the cement to shatter it, much to the chagrin of his mother and one of his aunts. "Really, Rue?" Wyatt's mother's tone was exasperated.

Rue just answered with that noncommittal shrug of hers,

like she didn't feel the need to explain herself to anybody, even the hostess.

After some effort, Wyatt got the card out. "Will this even work anymore?"

"You can use it online if it doesn't," Rue said.

He nodded like that was fair, stuck the wet card in his back pocket, and opened the next gift. I could tell his enthusiasm for a lot of them was feigned, though he seemed to genuinely like the Jazz tickets I got him. Courtney oohed over them and asked if she could be his date.

Rue shot me a glance. "How much were those?"

I answered with a noncommittal shrug. Honestly, Green Rabbit Solar paid me a really good salary and the cost of living in Utah wasn't bad, so it didn't really break the bank for me.

Once everything was opened and Wyatt had thanked everyone, his mom got up to add a final thank-you to the guests. People started wrangling their kids. Rue immediately bolted from her chair and moved to help pick up the mess, going first for wrapping paper and then for plates left on tables.

Keeping one eye on her, I approached Mrs. Thompson and shook her hand. "Great party. Thanks for inviting me." Though Wyatt had technically invited me.

"Oh, it's a pleasure!" She shook my hand with a strong grip. "You stop by anytime. Take him out to more places. He needs to meet more women."

I laughed to be polite—it was aggravating to have one's lack of romantic relationship success brought up again and again, and though she wasn't referring to me, there was a little bit of a sting there. She didn't mean anything by it. They never meant anything by it.

Turning around, I spied Rue pushing some upside-down plates into a very full garbage can and jogged over to help her. I pushed down too, compacting the trash and apparently startling her.

She pulled back. "Oh, thanks."

Nodding, I grabbed two ends of the large black trash bag and tied them together. "This is one heck of a party, eh?"

"It's a hot mess behind the scenes," she said, glancing toward the parking lot. "If she doesn't have a party to plan, she gets mopey."

It took a beat for me to catch that she meant Wyatt's mom. "She just cares about other people."

Her green eyes flicked back to me. "Yeah, I guess so." She touched one shoulder, then the other, locating the strap of her purse. "Well, I'm out."

She turned to leave.

"Hey, wait," I called, and she paused. Didn't turn around right away, so I stepped around the garbage can to face her. The red eyeshadow really brought out the green in her irises, and the setting sun highlighted the pink in her hair and on her cheeks. Pink cheeks were a good sign.

"So there's this neat little sushi place downtown that I just discovered. It has really good ratings." I stuffed my hands in my pockets, oddly nervous. Yeah, it wasn't super hard for me to get a *first* date, but I hadn't actually asked anyone out since things ended with TaLeah. It'd been a long and lonely year. "I'd love to take you sometime next week."

Her eyes widened a little more with each word, until they were the size of 3032 coin cell batteries. Her lips parted too, the gloss worn off. They looked soft—

"No."

My thoughts reeled back. "No?"

She blinked, and her eyes shrank back down, her eyebrows following them until a fine line formed between them. "Absolutely not."

She turned to go again. Shock held my tongue for half a second before I said, "Wait, really? Why?"

She whirled on me, nearly smacking her purse into my hip. "The fact that you don't know is the biggest reason I'm saying no."

She huffed and strode away, pink hair bobbing, leaving me in a stupor. I stared after her, gut falling, the uncomfortable yet familiar twinge of rejection prodding my chest. Had I read her so wrong? Had I lost my charm?

The fact that you don't know . . . What was I not picking up on? Maybe she wasn't into guys . . . but she'd just say as much, right? And she'd been at the singles mixer . . .

Why were women so complicated? Yet Rue had seemed so completely *un*complicated.

One of Wyatt's relatives stopped her to speak with her. I pulled my eyes away, a little uneasy. Trash can forgotten, I walked away, mulling over my every interaction with her, trying to figure out where I went wrong. Had I offended her with the LARP stuff? But it was just a joke. Maybe it was a really sensitive topic.

I eventually found myself by Wyatt, who was chatting with a couple of guys I didn't know. I lingered off to the side until they said their goodbyes. Didn't even need to explain myself—apparently my dejection was etched into my face.

"Dude," Wyatt said, suddenly serious, "what happened?"

I let out a mirthless chuckle. "Well, I just asked Rue out to dinner and got blatantly rejected."

He pulled back a little. Blinked. "Huh. Man, I'm sorry. She can be . . . prickly. Didn't think she was your type, to be honest."

"Apparently she isn't." I glanced across the pavilion—the man speaking with Rue had just departed. I ran a hand back through my hair. "I mean, does she like you? You guys have a history or something?"

Wyatt stared blankly at me. "What, like a *dating* history?"

"Yeah."

A laugh wheezed out of him, then another. Enough that he bent over for lack of air.

I didn't grasp what was so funny. "What?"

"Dude." He pressed a hand into his stomach, trying to regain his breath. "She's my *sister*."

Tingles went down my arm. "Sister?" My stomach knotted. "I thought you only had one sister—"

"Yeah"—he wiped his eye—"and that's her."

And suddenly, as every organ in my body detached and dropped to my feet, everything connected.

And I absolutely understood why Rue had said no.

RUE

Still unsettled, I watched Landry and Wyatt from across the pavilion after my uncle said his goodbyes and headed to his car. I couldn't wrap my head around it. I replayed Landry's proposition over and over in my head, wondering if I'd misunderstood, but he had clearly asked me on a date. Even now, revulsion warred with old, corpse-ridden want, which only acted as kindling to anger, because I did *not* want Landry Harrison. Wanting Landry was like a sack of trash wanting a garbage truck, despite knowing its fate.

I watched them, ready to leave, but then I saw it. I *knew* they were talking about me, and I *saw* it—the moment it clicked. The moment Samantha and Rue became one in Landry's mind. It was the moment that stupid sitcom smile dripped right off his face, and his pretty blue eyes widened with delicious mortification. The moment they turned and found me on the other side of the pavilion, shimmering even bluer as every last drop of blood drained out of his face, making him even paler than me.

In that moment, it was almost worth all the anger and hurt he put me through. The utter shock in his expression validated everything—that he knew what he'd done, and it'd just came back to bite him in the ass.

It was subtle, but it felt like victory.

Checkmate, hoser.

And with that delectable bit of social revenge, I spun on my heel and strode into the parking lot. Best if I got to bed early, anyway.

I had a LARP tomorrow, and I'd play all the freer with Landry Harrison freshly amputated from my story.

I totally know what you mean, about hope. Depresion or not, broken hope hurts all of us. But it makes us stronger in the end, you know? Can't understand all the good in the world if we don't likewise understand the bad. My mom would tell me that, whenever something bad happened (usually a bad score on a test or a dumb breakup, but you get the jist).

And yeah, thanks! I don't mind the ADHD jokes. They say all comedy comes from a place of hurt, but it's kind of like a medecine. Did I tell you it's on my bucket list to do standup one day? I think it'd be great, but I'm so scared! I think if I did a set and bombed I would have to crawl into a whole and live there until I was thirty. Or move to Canada. Or something. Ha ha.

Do you go to comedy clubs much? If not, I would love to take you. Only to a reputible one, of course. Unless you like the audience-high of sitting beside a serial killer while watching someone completly fail in a public setting . . .

Chapter 6

LANDRY

IN TRUTH, I deserved Rue's—Samantha's—cold shoulder. I'd earned it.

Here's the thing about Latter-day Saint missions. They're a wonderful experience. A great way to look outside yourself and genuinely desire to help others and grow closer to God. But the rules are strict, and after a while, people back home start to move on without you.

I'd always been a well-liked kid. When I had my farewell—my last day in church before setting out—I'd had friends from all over, and from all faiths, filling the pews. Friends who came to wish me well, to say goodbye, to send me off. A lot of those friends wrote me too. Mission rules meant that while I had a phone, I couldn't call home unless it was Christmas or Mother's Day. While I had a computer, I couldn't send personal emails.

After six months in the field, about two-thirds of my friends stopped writing me. They just didn't have the time, or forgot about it, or kept putting it off. Nothing malignant, really. I was not the center of their lives, and their lives moved on. By my year mark, I only had a biweekly letter from my parents, and occasionally one of my brothers, to go off of.

I was lonely.

But Elder Thompson—Wyatt—he had a diligent sister writing him. Not just a quick message either—several pages a week, full of words and jokes and drawings and photographs. Sometimes she sent care packages. She was so diligent, and he spoke so well of her. I saw some of her pictures. She was cute.

So I decided to write her. And to my delight, she wrote me too. Big, thick letters, just like the ones she sent her brother. Care packages came later—they were always personalized, and often on theme with the closest holiday. The shipping must have been a notable expense, especially for an undergrad.

And honestly, I'd liked her. Not just the paper-and-stamps company, but *her*. She was real, she was honest, and she was funny. Honestly, if so much time hadn't passed, I might have made the connection on personality alone, though Rue seemed more . . . I don't know, blasé than Samantha had been. But more sure of herself too.

So I wrote her. I sent her pictures of the mission. I told her about my life and my ambitions and listened to hers. I didn't have the letters anymore—there was a lot I had to leave in North Carolina that wouldn't fit in my suitcases. I'd even made plans with her for a number of things.

Then I got home, and suddenly everyone remembered me. My homecoming—first day in church after my return—all those friends came back. We hung out and caught up and shared stories. All that attention I'd missed during my two years away engulfed me, and I got completely lost in it.

I remember thinking, in the back of my mind, I should email

Samantha. Call her. She'd given me her contact information. But then my family would take me on vacation, or my high school friends wanted to see a movie, or the girl in my neighborhood I had a huge crush on broke up with her boyfriend and showed interest in me. Then there was getting everything ready for school, finding an apartment, getting back on the grid . . . I put it off. And put it off. And put it off.

Until enough time passed that it just felt weird to do anything about it.

Not an excuse. I am very aware now how poor of an excuse that was. But, despite dedicating two years to service, I was selfish and thought only of myself, and in a sad way, I didn't *need* Samantha Thompson anymore. So I let her go. So much so that when she walked back into my life, I didn't recognize her.

In my defense, I never knew her nickname. Then again, maybe if I hadn't ghosted her, I would have. But what was done was done, and I couldn't build a time machine and kick my twenty-one-year-old self, just like I couldn't zip back eighteen months and tell myself to stay the hell away from TaLeah.

I perked up, sitting on my sofa and looking out my bedroom window at the lights of Salt Lake City. I guess God *did* have a sense of humor, didn't he? Surely this couldn't all be happenstance.

TaLeah. TaLeah was to me what I'd been to Rue. I'd been drawn to her almost instantly. She was a few years my junior, tan and long-legged, pretty enough to grace the cover of any magazine. She was bubbly and assertive and funny. She was, I realized later, just like a salesman. And, as I learned through a mutual friend much later, she'd seen me as a conquest and took the challenge. I gave in pretty easily. I'd outgrown my skirt-chasing days, matured, and was ready to settle down. At first glance, TaLeah was everything I wanted. Heck, she was the female version of *me*.

We had a whirlwind romance. We saw each other nearly every day. We saw the premiere of every new movie, ate at every notable restaurant, even jumped out of a plane together. When I bought a ring and got down on one knee, she said yes. Posted it all over social media. Got bucketloads of that coveted thing: attention.

A week later, she called it off. Sudden and sharp, just like that. Posted it, again, all over social media, without a care as to how it would affect me. And again, she got bucketloads of attention.

Because attention was all TaLeah ever really wanted. And once I'd given her every iota I had, she moved on.

Never mind that it had shattered me.

I rubbed a hand down my face. It wasn't exactly the same, obviously. I'd never actually *dated* Samantha. But, though I'd never met her in person, we'd had a relationship. We'd been close. I'd shared things with her I didn't tell anyone else, and I knew she'd done the same with me. I wondered how it must have felt for her, when I stopped responding. It must have been bad, for her to still be so angry with me all these years later.

Married with kids. A thought I'd pasted into my brain to alleviate guilt. *Definitely not married with kids.*

I wondered if she actually went to that Renaissance faire or if she'd figured out what a loser I was beforehand. Nausea nestled in my stomach at the thought of her waiting for me. I hope she hadn't waited for me. I probably could have still accessed my LDSmail account to see if she'd contacted me there, but . . . it was definitely retired by now.

I let out a deep breath and stared out toward the capitol building. Rue had been the first woman I'd asked out since my ex-fiancée obliterated me on Facebook and Snapchat. And I'd been rightfully rejected.

But . . . I liked her. I really did. Given that time machine, I really would go back in time and remind my stupid younger self to call her up. Give her a chance. Maybe the stars still wouldn't have aligned, but at least I wouldn't feel like such a dolt now.

And honestly, I wasn't sure what to do. Nothing, for now. She was obviously pissed at me and needed some space. But I was pretty sure the Samantha from those old letters liked me, so if I could convince her to forgive me, maybe the Rue of today would give me a second chance. I had to try. Quitting wasn't really my style.

She was the first woman in a year to spark anything in me.

There was at least one step I could take. Pulling out my phone, I opened my text messages and clicked on Wyatt's name.

> Hey man, could I get your sister's number?

Anything more would have to wait.

RUE

I rammed into my own teammates *hard*.

I took the blockers by surprise, but they dug their brakes into the waxed floor and pushed back, careful to watch their hands. This was only a practice, but we still played like we were in an actual game, even though we had no referee present to call us out on foul play. Dancing on my own brakes, I feinted left, then slid through an opening on the right, barely squeezing through to open track. I sped around the ring, pushing my skates out, forcing my quads to work. Speed wasn't crucial for this, but I was on edge, and hurting my body gave me something else to think about.

By the time derby practice was over, I was drenched in sweat, huffing, and pretty sure I'd pulled a tendon or two.

"Nice moves today," Yolanda said as I yanked off my skates. "We're going to crush the Pleasant Graves."

I smiled and shrugged. "The Pleasant Graves aren't hard to crush."

"Crush to a *pulp*," Emily, another blocker, amended for Yolanda.

I nodded my agreement. A win, even an easy win, would cheer me up. "Definitely. See you guys Saturday."

They waved, and I took my time packing away my skates and pads. I'd been on edge for four days, ever since Wyatt's birthday party. Ever since Landry asked me out. Like, *actually asked me out.*

I didn't know what to do with that. In the moment, it felt good to tell him no. It felt amazing to see his stupid face when he finally engaged his brain and realized who I was. But then why did I feel so . . . *off* about it? I was angry, not satisfied. And I kept picking at it like a crusty scab. Maybe because eight years ago my naive heart would have bloomed to hear those words from Landry's lips. Eight years ago, I'd expected it. He was the knight in shining armor I'd always wanted, and I'd been left in the tower with the evil witch. Maybe because a private humiliation wasn't enough balm for my wounds. Maybe I should have made a show of it. Shouted and danced in all my red-sequin glory.

Or maybe because Landry had seemed so genuine about it, and I felt ~~hurt~~ guilty, which was stupid.

"I am *not* paying for therapy over this." I shoved my disposable water bottle—which I refused to dispose of out of sheer laziness—into my bag. "*He* should pay for therapy for this."

I should send him a bill. If I'd had his home address, I might have sent him one eight years ago.

That was the other frustrating thing. I was *over* this. I was! It sucked, but the wound scarred and healed and I talked it out and I moved on. Landry Harrison hadn't occupied my thoughts—much—for years, until I saw that ominous letter in my old bedroom closet. But I'd done my time in heartbreak jail, and it wasn't fair to make me stare at the bars again. It *wasn't fair*, and it was *all his fault*.

I was the last to leave practice. My stuff was put away, my sweat was dry, my helmet swung from the strap of my bag. I sat there on the gymnasium floor, staring at chipped varnish for a while, not particularly thinking about anything, just feeling. A weird sort of meditation where I just shut off a little bit.

Then I stood up, grabbed my crap, killed the lights, and locked up. Regardless of my subconscious salad, I could at least take respite in knowing it was finally over. There was no way Landry Harrison would come within ten miles of me now.

Hope he had fun paying the fines on that library book, in that case.

Saturday couldn't come fast enough. Not just for the derby game, but for the next LARP session. Anastene was working on a puzzle, and I was sure Rhonda was going to divulge a few more pieces of it today. She was so good at plot, and I was positive this session had something to do with Anastene's backstory. Maybe finding the mother who walked out on her as a kid or the pirate who cheated her one year before the present story line started, robbing her of all her wealth and forcing her to start over from scratch. (Thus her reasoning for joining up with the other characters and playing this campaign. Motivation is important!)

I'd made myself a new sword this week out of a carbon fiber tube, EVA foam, and an awesome sleeve I crafted from some silver fabric I found. It was so bright it looked like aluminum foil. It was a little longer than the one I currently had, which would help in combat, but I had to drop it off at the market and earn it in-game before I could use it. Then each of my hits would do three damage instead of two.

Mmmm . . . delicious foam murder.

With that set up, I tightened the laces on my gauntlets and trekked over to the giant oak tree where the others were gathered, a grin on my face and a bounce to my step. I wanted to get started right away. Rhonda had left us on a cliff hanger, and I was dying to know what happened next, even without my little puzzle side quest. Cameron nodded to me. It was Cameron, not Drakon, because we hadn't started the game yet. He seemed a little tense. I wondered if Rhonda had just assigned him a mission he wasn't thrilled with.

She'd just finished instructing the high schoolers, because all three ran off, tying yellow ribbons to their arms to indicate they were NPCs. Adelaide leaned over to whisper something to Thom. I squeezed in between Thom and McKenzie and leaned on my foam sword.

"And this one is new to the game, so go easy on him," Rhonda said without lifting her eyes from the clipboard, jutting her thumb to her right. "Today we're starting in Tromadon Market—"

My eyes flitted over to the new player and nearly toppled out of my head like a couple of d20s.

Landry's blue eyes met mine, and he smiled.

"What the actual—" I said out loud, interrupting Rhonda.

Lifting her head, she raised an eyebrow at me.

I literally didn't know what to say. I stood there with my mouth open, frozen, my veins knitting themselves into senseless shapes and my breakfast shifting low in my gut.

Landry . . . was here. At the park. *In my LARP game.*

No. *No no no no no no no no no.* Not here. Anywhere but here. LARP was my safe space. *Get the flying eff out of my safe space!*

"And remember, no killing in the cities," Rhonda finished, tucking her board away. She handed Landry a wooden box about the length of my forearm.

"And I just go over there?" he asked.

She nodded. "You'll get the hang of it."

Landry smiled at me one more time before jogging over to another area, separate from Henry and his friends.

And I just stood there, gaping, while the others walked to the playground, a.k.a. our city.

"R-Rhonda," I said, grabbing her sleeve as she passed by. "Why is he here?"

She glanced over to Landry. "He signed up online yesterday. You know him?"

A million curse words tangled in my throat. "Friend of a friend," I growled. "But he's only NPCing, right?"

She nodded.

"Can you tell him we're full or something? Make him leave?" If he didn't pay dues, we didn't owe him anything.

Her eyes narrowed on me. "Has he done anything illegal in regards to your person that I need to know about?"

Grimacing, I shook my head.

She shrugged. "Then I'm not kicking him out. We need more players. Leave your personal issues at home." She slapped me on the shoulder and smirked. "I promise it will be worth it."

She strode toward the playground. Working my fists, steeling myself, I stomped over to Landry.

He saw me and, in an absolutely terrible British accent, said, "Hello, fair maiden. I—"

"Cut the crap," I snapped. "First of all, I'm not a maiden, I'm a rogue. Second of all, you don't belong here."

He frowned. "Pretty sure the website says, 'All are welcome.'"

I threw my hands up in the air. "What is your deal? You don't LARP."

"I do now."

I scowled. "You *don't*."

"You made it sound fun!" His tone was so lighthearted I wanted to stab it with a poisoned arrow. He must have sensed it, because his expression sobered. "Hey, I thought I'd give it a try. I'm sorry—I didn't realize it would bother you so much."

I rolled my eyes. "I'm sure."

"And Rue"—he lowered the box he was holding—"about the letters. I'm really—"

I pointed a finger at him so swiftly I nearly scratched his nose. "Don't," I snapped, and whirled back to catch up with the others.

There was no way he'd come here to ask me out again. No way. So why? To apologize for wrecking me eight years ago? Almost a decade too late, dude.

I tried really hard to focus on the story. Focus and earn a few more gems so I could buy my new sword.

I didn't do a very good job of it.

LANDRY

I was a little surprised by how intense LARPing was.

People only introduced themselves as their character names. Their costumes were stellar—lots of leatherworking, stitching, feathers, weapons . . . I mean, the weapons were a little silly, but I understood they couldn't play with real swords.

My job, so Rhonda told me, was to play an old monk, and the copse of trees I was in represented a temple. *Theater of the mind,* she explained. Which essentially meant I was playing pretend with grown-ups. I'd thought today would be the most awkward day of my life, but when everyone else around me was so in character, it felt stranger not to play along. She'd given me a robe to put over my clothes so I'd match the image a little more. It smelled like cats.

Even Rue, who'd given me enough death glares to kill a small animal, stayed in character when she had to interact with me. She came with another guy who called himself Drakon and walked around the entire copse of trees before approaching me. She had a slight lilt to her voice when she spoke. But it wasn't like the "Southern" woman at the singles mixer. It didn't feel like a lie or a device. It just added flavor. Increased immersion.

Admittedly, it was kind of hot.

"What is your name?" Rue—Anastene, if I heard her character's name correctly—asked.

I had a card at my hip with my information on it, but I'd read it over dozens of times while waiting for the story line to reach me. "I am Angus the Blue, fair . . . my lady," I said, remembering her calling me out when I'd said "fair maiden" earlier.

Drakon—hadn't caught his real name yet—stepped in front of her. "What do you look like?"

I wasn't sure if he was asking me or my character. "Uh"—I thought of the card—"I'm an old human male." Then, trying to do an accent, I added, "I am keeper of this temple."

"This temple is in shambles," Rue said, looked around with a twist to her mouth. I didn't remember Rhonda saying anything about the temple being junky. "You must be a poor keeper."

I tried to think of an adequate response. Amusement flashed in her eyes.

Oh, right. She hated me. Of course she would make this hard. But I enjoyed a challenge.

"I keep that which is important," I replied, trying to channel every fantasy movie I'd ever seen into the act, which, admittedly, wasn't many. "Like this." I hefted the box.

Drakon reached to take it, but Rue stopped him. "No. It might be a trap."

It wasn't a trap.

She met my eyes, her own hard. "He may be trying to trick us."

Drakon's gaze flashed between Rue and me, but he played along. "You think?"

"Yes." She pulled out a short foam stick that I was pretty sure was a dagger. "Lower the box, *keeper*."

Rhonda had been firm that I shouldn't give the box over easily unless someone mentioned the name Hentwig. "I can't do that," I said, forgetting to use my accent.

Drakon put his hand on the hilt of his fake hammer and puffed up his chest in a way that maybe was supposed to look cool. "Methinks you best listen to the lady."

"What's going on here?" Another woman jogged up. Her costume was light, leatherworked, and studded with a few fake flowers. "We've been searching for you. Anastene, why is your dagger drawn?"

See? Dagger. I know things.

"This menace is acting the part of a temple keeper, but he lies. He's a mercenary working for Aylock."

I had absolutely no idea what she meant. "No," I interjected, "I—"

"*Silence!*" Drakon bellowed.

I had no idea what to do with myself. Maybe drop the box and run, but I didn't know if Rhonda would kick me out if I didn't follow her instructions.

The new woman looked around. "Are you sure?"

"Positive." Rue smirked. She bolted forward and hit my left hand with her foam dagger.

I stood there. "Um . . ."

The newcomer said, "You lost your hand."

"Oh, right." I dropped my hand, but the box was small enough that I could still hold it with my right. "Ow, why would you do that," I said, less enthusiastic about my character. The whole idea I'd had to warm up to Rue by engaging in her hobbies was not going as well as it would if this were a chick flick. The movies had lied to me.

Drakon snatched the box from my hand. "If there is anything menacing in this box, your life is forfeit." He held it against his stomach and stared at it dramatically. For way longer than should be normal.

"Um," I tried, but was ignored.

Rue's eyes pulled from me to Drakon. Her forehead sparkled with glittery scales. TaLeah would never have gone anywhere in public with something like that outside of Halloween. Actually . . . I didn't think any of the girls I'd dated would have.

"We could wait for Johnny," she said.

I was pretty sure that was the tall Chinese guy with a purple sash tied to his arm. He didn't have any foam weapons on him, but he "cast spells" every once in a while.

"No," Drakon said with such ferocity I rolled my eyes. "I will do it. I will suffer the consequences."

Oh, give me a break. I'd already looked in the box. It only held a couple plastic gems and a piece of paper than had been burned on the edges with a lighter to make it look old.

Drakon held his breath. Opened the box.

"Curse?" Rue asked.

He shook his head. Pulled out the gems and gave a third of them to Rue, and another third to the other woman. Setting the box down, he read the message. "It's a poem. It speaks of the Winter Forests and a dancer with a jewel on her brow."

"Isn't Hentwig's sister a sky dancer?" Rue asked.

Isn't a sky dancer a toy from the nineties? I thought, but remembered myself. "Ah, you know Hentwig—"

"Shush," Rue snapped without looking my way. "Let's take this back to the others."

Drakon and Newcomer nodded and ran away from the trees, leaving me with an empty box and a cue card of information I hadn't had a chance to relate.

I sighed and sat down, pulling out my phone.

Quitting didn't sound like such a bad idea.

Elder Harrison,
I was wondering how long it would take for you to start preaching to me. Just kidding.
I don't know. Yeah, I do believe in God, but maybe I'm not settled on how or what God is? Like is it an all-powerful force permeating everything in our lives, or maybe just the lives of good people? But what makes a person "good"? I mean, I've seen The Ten Commandments *and all that jazz, and we all have a moral compass, but there's a lot of churches and such that draw a lot of different lines that intersect in weird ways, if that makes sense. Or maybe God is a person. Or two people. Or ten. But yeah, there's something out there. I'm taking a biology course and sometimes I think none of this stuff could just happen on its own, you know? It's too bizarre.*

Chapter 7

RUE

A RAVEN (IMAGINARY) delivered me the next clue to Anastene's puzzle, so during downtime when everyone was checking out their own side quests and making purchases in our "city," I sat at a picnic table and unrolled my note. It was in code, but I'd received a cipher weeks earlier. I smiled at the chance to finally use it and see what the story had in store for me.

Cameron/Drakon sat down by me with his LARP journal open. "What does it say?" he asked.

"'Don't trust' is all I have so far." I scanned the cipher for a symbol that looked like a snake's head. Found it, wrote down an *A*.

"Hey"—he spoke a little lower—"what's the deal with the new guy? Robert?"

"Landry." I glanced up from my cipher and searched the area for him. He was talking to Rhonda again, smiling his perfect toothpaste-ad smile, as always. He was so confusing—he seemed genuinely happy, despite obviously being out of his element, and despite me and Cameron's less-than-friendly encounter with him earlier. It wasn't an act—he'd always been like that. Cheerful and well-meaning. I remember when he wrote me after being mugged in North Carolina. He'd seemed jazzed to have an interesting story to share, never mind that he'd lost his driver's license and spending money.

I shrugged and resumed decoding my message. "He's not my favorite person, let's put it that way."

"Hmm." Cameron turned and watched him for a moment as I wrote down *N* and *Y*.

"There's rumor in the city that bandits are afoot. He might be one of them," he said, standing half in character and half out.

I shrugged. "Maybe. Rhonda usually has the kids do that."

"But we might have a hard time telling them all apart. You know. If you want to murder him."

I couldn't help the smirk rising to my face. Pausing my translation, I met Cameron's eyes. "I think that is a fantastic idea."

He beamed like I'd just told him he'd won the Nobel Peace Prize. Nerd.

A minute later, he dipped his head toward my work. "What does it say?"

I lifted my paper. "'Don't trust any creature who smiles while you cry.'"

"Huh." He pulled some fruit leather from one of the pouches around his waist. "Want some?"

I shook my head, looking over the message. I had a hunch it had something to do with the pirate in Anastene's backstory, and I wondered how literally I was meant to take it.

Glancing up, I found Rhonda arming Landry with a foam

shield and sword, and realized the advice was painfully true to real life as well.

LANDRY

Man. Foam swords can hurt when you put enough effort into the swing.

I'd wheedled out everyone's names, thanks to Henry, a fifteen-year-old who was Rhonda's nephew. Johnny, McKenzie, Adelaide, and Thom were all fine, but Cameron—the oaf who harassed me when I played the monk—and Rue swung at me like I was trying to murder a litter of newborn puppies. And being an NPC, as soon as I died, I had to "respawn" as a new character to be wailed upon, so I'd gotten smacked around quite a bit. Players were yelling out their damage so quickly I couldn't even keep up with the math. I just knew when it had definitely gone over ten, and I dropped dramatically to the ground, playing corpse for about five seconds before shuffling out of the way. Or sometimes I just dropped with my arms covering my head to spare myself some bruises.

Playing an NPC got me points to put toward playing a PC, or a main character. It was a way to save money, since every session cost twenty bucks. But after taking a few hundred blows and being targeted by the woman I was *trying* to impress and the bloke obviously trying to do the same, I was ready to fork out the cash to play the main story.

We returned to the "town" or whatever after the battle, and I changed into what was essentially a burlap sack with arm holes cut out of it. The little card Rhonda handed me said I was a peasant named Gunther who had no money and thus could not send anyone on quests, but I had information on the local crime lord, so if someone asked me and was willing to give up a couple gems, I could share that with them. I stuck the card in the back pocket of my jeans to ensure no one gleaned the information unfairly.

Looking at you, Cameron.

Ironically, Rue was the first one to approach me. She didn't look happy about it, but she also didn't try to twist my character around and find an excuse to, I don't know, cut off one of my extremities.

"You," she said, somewhat warily, "what's your name?"

"Gunther," I responded matter-of-factly.

"Do you know anything about who's bribing the mayor?"

I folded my arms. "For someone trying to get information about the underbelly, you sure are talking loud."

Her eyebrow crooked slightly. Was she impressed? Folding her arms, she matched my pose. "For someone playing a lowly peasant, you sure are being difficult."

I bit down on a smile, and I was pretty sure she did too. I'd take it.

"The only person with enough money to do that is Hophs, the crime lord. He goes to the Silver Spoon for dinner on Wednesdays."

She nodded. Handed me a couple yellow gems—which was good, because I'd forgotten to ask for them. Her money pouch was a quilted pattern of brown and green leather, making it look like some overripe, exotic mango.

"Hey," I said, stepping out of character. So far I hadn't seen anyone penalized for it. "Your costume is pretty amazing."

She rolled her eyes. "Thanks."

"Really, though. The braidwork on the edge of the skirt is pretty cool." I didn't know what type of braid it was—the kind that made a bunch of sharp, overlying triangles. It blended in with the skirt, both of them black, but it had subtle highlights of maroon and that same pink from her pouch.

She paused. "Oh. Thanks." She touched the border. "No one ever notices that. It took me hours."

I nodded. "I believe it. My fingers are too clumsy to even try."

I offered her a smile, and while she didn't return it, there was no venom in her gaze when she met mine, and that was enough for me.

RUE

So *what* if he noticed the braiding?

I drove to my parents' new house in Lindon Sunday evening for family dinner, which they tried to host at least once a month. I winced stepping out of my car—between enthusiastic role-playing and a slightly more intense game than usual against the Pleasant Graves last night, my quads and calves were feeling it today.

I was the last to arrive, and my mom greeted me like she hadn't seen me all year, calling out my name and giving me a big hug in the front room.

"Yeah, yeah, I love you too. Sheesh." I pulled from her grasp and looked around. The front room, at least, was entirely put together after their move. "It looks really nice, Mom." I spun, taking it in. "Did you restain the piano?"

"Nope! Just better lighting." She shimmied over to the window to adjust the blinds so more evening light would pour through them. "But the rug is new! What do you think?"

I looked down at a white braided rug. "I think I should take my shoes off."

"Oh, would you?"

"Yeah." I slipped off my Converse and set them by the door. "But it looks really nice. Really open." Maybe I could get a white rug. Not that anyone ever saw the inside of my house.

The thought made me miss Blaine, but I couldn't blame her for leaving. My mom and I definitely had our differences, but if she lived in another state and got sick, I'd probably pick up my life to help her out too. She'd do the same for me. My whole family would.

With that warm fuzzy nestled in my precious heart, I followed Mom into the small dining room. The table was only large enough for four, but we only had four, until Wyatt got hitched or something, which wasn't happening anytime soon. The kitchen was smaller as well, but that was the point of downsizing. My dad and Wyatt were already sitting on the table, debating over something about Moses.

"And now we switch to an *interesting* topic," I said as I sat down, letting my purse drop unceremoniously to the floor behind me. "Like fly-fishing."

My dad perked up. "Have you gotten into fly-fishing?"

Wyatt snorted. "It's a joke, Dad. Can you see Rue wading out in a cold river to catch fish?"

I shrugged. "Wouldn't be the worst."

"How was your game yesterday?" Dad asked. He and

mom usually came to the first game of the season to be supportive, but derby wasn't really their thing. To be honest, it wasn't really 99.5 percent of the state's "thing."

"We won," I said, absently rubbing my sore thigh.

"Good, good," Mom said as she brought a small roast chicken over and set it in the middle of the table.

My stomach rumbled. "Thanks, Mom. It smells really good."

"We're happy to help, you know," Wyatt pressed. It wasn't the first time we'd had this conversation. "We can bring sides."

"Not necessary." Mom shook her head and took her seat. Mom had a gluten allergy, and she didn't trust anyone—even her own flesh and blood—to not accidentally poison her with a potluck. Which reminded me that I still needed to sign up for Herospect's.

We said grace and dug into the food, me and Wyatt shouldering each other as we both darted for the chicken's legs. Best part of a roast chicken, no contest.

"There's one for each of you, you animals!" Mom swatted at Wyatt with an oven glove.

I laughed and yanked off my leg, taking the thigh with it. My dad sighed and carved the rest of the mutilated bird while Wyatt and I reverted to children and fought over mashed potatoes, gravy, rolls, and green beans.

"How's work?" Dad asked. He'd recently retired, himself.

"Good." Wyatt said around half a mouthful of chicken. "We just got a new client in the fashion business, so that'll be interesting."

Mom chuckled. "And what do you know about fashion?"

Wyatt shrugged. "I don't need to know anything about it outside of how to sell it."

Dad glanced over for my answer.

I shrugged. "Literally the same response I always give. I type stuff into outdated software and send it off."

Dad mentioned a neighbor with a new start-up hiring, insinuating Wyatt might want to look into it, but Wyatt insisted he was comfortable where he was. Mom asked about church to be polite, then asked about any new young women in Wyatt's life. She did not turn the conversation over to me to ask about young men. She just didn't think about it, I know, but sometimes I wondered if my mom considered me a lost cause. In her book, I wouldn't get married until (a) I went back to my natural hair color, (b) I grew it out, and (c) I fixed my "attitude problem."

"I'm tagging along with Landry's ward this week to float the Provo River," Wyatt said, and I bit the inside of my cheek at the mention of his name. "I'm sure there will be lots of pickings there."

I swallowed. "Because that's what women want you to call them."

My comment was overlooked, or possibly not heard. "Oh, Landry!" Mom said. "He's such a nice young man."

"Do we have to talk about Landry?" I stabbed a green bean. Nothing was sacred anymore.

"Yeah, his complex has a really nice pool that we've gotten to use a couple times," Wyatt said.

Mom shook her head as she mixed her mashed potatoes. "I don't know how that one isn't married yet."

Wyatt shrugged. "Apparently he was engaged in Florida."

I stiffened and glanced at my brother.

"He was?" My mother's well-manicured hand went to her chest. "What happened?"

"Ended, obviously."

"Not surprised," I muttered. "He breaks lots of things."

"Oh, come on, Rue." The hard edge in Wyatt's voice caught me off guard. "What is your deal with him?"

"What deal?" Mom asked as Dad silently buttered a roll.

"I don't have a *deal*," I retorted.

"Obviously you do. He's a good guy. Give him a break," Wyatt said.

"What deal?" Mom repeated.

I stared bullets at Wyatt. *Don't you dare tell her he asked me out.* I would never hear the end of it.

Wyatt bristled but refocused on his food. "Nothing. It's nothing." He set down his fork and grabbed his roll. "But," he added, "for your information, he didn't 'break' anything. She dumped him."

I picked at a cuticle. "Oh." The information should have bolstered me, made me feel vindicated, but it didn't. It made me . . . I honestly didn't know. Jittery. Swallowing my pride, I asked, "What happened?"

He shrugged, not meeting my eyes. "I don't know. He didn't really want to talk about it."

I let out a long breath. "Sorry."

"Hmm."

"No, really," I tried, pushing against my risen defensiveness and taking a good internal look at myself. Why had I said that? Why was I dallying with so much poison? "I'm sorry, Wyatt."

He focused on his roll, but he'd forgive me by the time the meal was over. Wyatt wasn't a grudge-keeper.

"How 'bout them Yankees, huh?" Dad asked.

Nobody responded.

Landry's dive into LARPing was not a one-time thing. He came back the next week. Without a yellow sash, which meant he'd coughed up the twenty bucks to be a PC, a playing character. The ones involved in the main story line, despite the fact that our story line was almost over.

I gawked at him when he came to the park. I just didn't *get* it. He was coming for me. That was clear. Unless he actually did magically fall in love with LARPing after NPCing one time, which I highly doubted. But . . . why? Why now? Why did he care *now*?

He showed up in what I supposed was the best costume a non-nerdy adult man could put together. He was wearing a vest and khakis and had tied two leather belts around his shoulders so they crossed over his chest. Oversize white dress shirt underneath, which I imagined he'd borrowed from someone. The finished look was quintessentially Mr. Darcy lost in the jungle.

I watched him from the corner of my eye when we gathered around Rhonda to start. Seamlessly blending our new player into the story, she explained, "Unfortunately, your wagon wheel has busted on the way to Kinlarda."

"Oh, come on," Cameron muttered. He seemed even less enthusiastic about Landry than I was.

"The closest town is still Tromadon," she continued. "But if you look northward, you see distant fire smoke."

"How far off does the smoke seem to be?" Johnny/Rell, our wizard, asked.

"To you?" A sly smile touched Rhonda's lips. She always

played to our characters' weaknesses. It helped us to bond together as a party. "Not far."

Adelaide/Justine, who had ranger skills, asked, "How far does it look to *me*?"

"About three miles," Rhonda answered.

Thom/Dyrek stuck his hands in his pockets. "It's about fourteen miles back to Tromadon." He glanced to our dungeon master for confirmation. She nodded.

I worked my mouth. I knew what this was. That campfire—maybe chimney fire—was going to lead us to Landry's character, because it made no sense going back to Tromadon for help. It would add twenty-eight miles to our journey, and Rhonda was a realist. She would make us take up extra game time if we did that.

My gaze slid to Landry. He looked so damn hopeful. I rolled my eyes.

"There's more supplies in Tromadon," I offered.

Thom/Dyrek looked at me like I was insane. "Yeah, and we already got them." He pointed like he could actually see the distant smoke. "If we can see that from three miles out, it's either a large party or another village, someone who can help us. Six miles is better than twenty-eight."

I nodded. I wasn't going to make my character completely incompetent to stick it to Landry. Unfortunately, paying his fee meant I *had* to interact with him. *Focus on the game,* I chided myself. "All right. Justine and I can check it out, if you want to watch the wagon." Not because I wanted to include Landry with open arms, but Justine and Anastene were the characters least likely to be detected, in case Rhonda pulled a fast one on us and intended us to walk into a horde of bandits or the like.

Rhonda nodded at Landry, who jogged off toward the playground. She handed a die to Johnny/Rell and told him to roll it every two minutes and record the number—she'd use it to determine what events, if any, happened with the watch party when we got back. Then she led me and Justine through the trees.

"What if there's no wainwright?" Justine asked.

I shrugged. "Then we put what we can in our packs and move on. Sell the rest."

Admittedly, my mind was only half in the story. The other half was annoyingly stuck on Landry.

I wondered who this woman was in Florida. Landry seemed like . . . not a *player*, but someone who liked to sample everything at a restaurant, you know? So what kind of woman had convinced him to settle down? What kind of job did she have? Introvert or extrovert? What were her hobbies or personality? Was she pretty?

Of course she was pretty, my thoughts pressed. Justine checked our surroundings before Rhonda led us on, circling back toward the playground. And the stupid question entered my head, *If I had been prettier, would he have called?*

I rolled my eyes and tried to focus on the game. Told Rhonda I was listening for anyone hiding in the trees. There were none. We closed in on the playground. There was one kid playing on it; we usually just ignored them.

But still, I wondered. What if Landry hadn't ghosted me? What if he'd come to the Renaissance faire? What if he'd kept all his promises? Where would we be now?

Well, there were two answers to that, as far as I was concerned. We'd either be married in a cottage down by the river or I'd still hate him, just for different reasons.

I shook my head, hoping my frustration wasn't evident to the others.

What did Rue have that Samantha lacked? Or was this just to appease his own guilt?

Were our roles reversed, I'd just avoid him. It wasn't hard. Salt Lake Valley and its connecting counties were full of places and people. Easy to get lost.

So get lost, Landry.

We reached the playground. Once we stepped on the bark chips surrounding the equipment, Landry started panto-miming . . . I couldn't tell. Was he raking or splitting logs?

"You see a small ranch house up ahead," Rhonda explained. "The smoke is billowing out of the chimney. A man in his late twenties is outside, moving feed bags from a wagon to his porch. His wagon is the same model as yours."

Of course it is. "Does he see us?" I asked.

"Not yet."

I glanced to Justine. "Not many other choices," she offered, setting her hand on the hilt of her foam sword. "Worst-case scenario, there's two of us and one of him."

I nodded, almost drawing my dagger—but as much as I'd love to pretend-gut Landry Harrison, Anastene wouldn't draw unless she was threatened. I left the foam accessory at my hip.

Adelaide/Justine walked forward first. "Ho, stranger!" She put up both hands. "We come as friends. Our party's vehicle has broken down on the main road. We're willing to trade for assistance."

"Oh hi!" he said, then cleared his throat and, in a Scottish accent, said, "Welcome, weary travelers!"

I rolled my eyes. He was stiff as a week-old sweatband.

He stood there, apparently unsure what to do next. Rhonda merely watched her clipboard. She didn't interfere unless she had to, which made her a great dungeon master, but . . .

I threw Landry a bone. "I hope your enthusiasm means you're willing to work with us?" I dropped the words in Anastene's subtle dialect.

"Oh yes, of course." His accent leaned a little more Welsh now. "Always happy to help. Um."

Cue another awkward pause.

Adelaide kindly offered, "My name is Justine, and this is my friend Anastene. One of our wheels has broken." She gestured to the invisible wagon outside the invisible ranch house. "Gods be praised, it takes the same size as yours. Do you have a spare wheel we could trade for? We've money on our persons, but more goods back at our cart."

Now, if I were playing Landry's character, I would insist on some act of goodwill—payment or the like—to ensure I wasn't being lured into a trap. But Landry simply said, "Oh yeah, I'll roll one out to you. I have two spares." He looked to Rhonda, perhaps for confirmation, but she was writing something down. "Um. Yes, let's go!"

I shifted my weight to one leg and folded my arms. "Your name?"

"Oh!" American accent. "It's Londry." Back to Scottish.

I gaped. Out of character, I said, "Your character's name is Laundry?"

"L-O-N-D-R-Y," he said, also out of character. He shrugged. "I wanted something I wouldn't forget."

Rhonda finally interjected, "So you're walking back with them?"

"Yes, ma'am," Landry/Londry replied.

She waved us over. "Come on, back we go."

I started back to the others first, eager to move on, but my steps gradually slowed as the situation chafed. My steps slowed, allowing Justine and Rhonda to get ahead of me. Begrudgingly, I fell into step beside Landry.

"Listen. First rule of thumb, relax," I offered, speaking normally.

He smiled gratefully at me. He had a Cupid's-bow lip and a strong jaw that acted like a gilded frame for that Christmas-card smile. Something about it made my stomach hurt. "Thanks. I, uh"—he laughed—"might be a little out of my depth."

"I noticed." I tried to shake the flatness in my tone. "Okay, what class are you?"

"Am I allowed to tell you that?"

I smacked him. "*Yes*, you're allowed to tell me that! We're team members!"

His eyes lit up at that, and I wanted to hit him for real. "I'm a paladin. Or I was. It's all backstory. I—"

"Don't tell me backstory." I glanced ahead to gauge how much time we had. "Okay, so paladins are servants of a specific god. They're very religious. So remember you're going to see everything through a religious lens, unless you left because you're jaded or something. But all that backstory should influence how you act."

He nodded.

"Make sure you have a clear goal and motivation. Keep them in the front of your mind at all times."

"My goal is to join the party."

"Not enough. *Londry* needs a goal. What does he want?

If you were writing a book, what does your character want more than anything else, and what is he willing to do to get it?"

Landry pressed his lips together, considering.

"Then"—I was almost out of time—"I would pick three major character details. Personality. Just focus on those three, and the rest will come naturally. Write them down, if that helps. Lastly, it's okay to lose. This isn't real life. No one actually dies."

He grinned at me, his face turning smoldery. "So that means you can't actually kill me."

I got caught staring at his eyes for a second before what he said registered. I shook myself. "Yeah, duh. Don't be dumb."

Flustered, I jogged ahead to meet our group and let Adelaide/Justine take over the negotiations. Landry floundered a little, especially when Cameron/Drakon played the skeptic to his good intentions, but then he did something that surprised me.

"On one condition."

"Name it," Thom/Dyrek said.

"I need to get to the next city," Landry/Londry pressed. "Personal business. Dangerous traveling this road alone. It would be safer in a group."

"Done," said Dyrek.

"Wait," interjected Drakon. "Which city?"

Rhonda interjected, "Londry wishes to go to Apple Reef, which is ten miles west of Kinlarda."

Drakon/Cameron stomped his foot. "That's out of the way! We don't have the time!"

"We're not going anywhere if we don't get this wheel," Adelaide/Justine countered.

Drakon shook his head. "No deal—"

"Deal," I interrupted, and Drakon nearly snapped his neck turning toward me. I sized up Londry. "You have fighting skill?"

He nodded and touched a foam sword—one of the spares Rhonda brought—strapped to his back. "Two-damage."

Not how the character would or should say it, but I nodded. "We can afford the stop. We can't afford to leave ourselves vulnerable to wolves, bandits, and orcs." I eyed Drakon, who looked like I'd just betrayed him, but I think that was more of a weird Cameron thing.

"Agreed," said Dyrek. "Welcome aboard, Londry."

After another half an hour, Landry managed to loosen up. The high-schooler NPCs played orcs and gave us a good fight, and at Apple Reef, Londry was able to get us into a temple, where we got healing for free. Part of his backstory apparently tied in with Chaylock's, McKenzie's character. And it was . . . fun.

I'd forgotten how easy it was to be pulled in by Landry Harrison. Letters were one thing, but real life? The draw was ten times stronger.

And it worried me.

LANDRY

This was . . . good.

I hesitated to think it, but today had gone *really* well. It took me a second to get into things, but I thought I pulled off my paladin pretty well—no one was complaining, anyway. At least, not to my face. And Rue was relaxing around me. Talking to me, in and out of character. *Helping* me.

Best twenty bucks I'd ever spent.

I grabbed her sword for her when everyone started packing up, though it barely weighed anything, being made primarily of foam. "Let me walk you to your car."

She glanced at me, her green eyes highlighted by the navy and violet glitter of her makeup. She dipped her head toward the parking lot and started walking. Another victory. I quickened my step to keep up, ignoring a scowl from—you guessed it—Cameron as I went.

Dude needed to relax.

"So I take it back," I said when we reached asphalt.

"Which thing?" she asked. Her focus lingered on a red Nissan Pathfinder. It shouldn't surprise me in the slightest that Rue drove a red car. It'd probably be pink if it was included in the dealership's standard lineup.

"The LARPing thing, at the ice cream joint," I clarified. "It's actually pretty fun."

"Of course it is." Her lip ticked up a little. "You'll come to learn that I'm right about most things."

"Are you now?"

She opened her hatchback; there was an overstuffed plastic grocery bag full of other grocery bags inside, probably intended to be recycled, and a clear tote that looked to be full of sewing stuff, duct tape, and other knickknacks. She dropped her arm bracers in, and I slid the sword beside them. She merely cast me a knowing glare, and something about it made my chest tighten.

"Thanks for helping me out too," I said.

She shrugged. "I hate seeing dumb animals suffer." But she wasn't able to fight the smile as much this time. Two dimples threatened to pop on her cheeks. The sight of it, with all her mermaidesque makeup, made her look like some sort of siren, beautiful and bizarre. Entrancing.

Okay, here went nothing.

"So," I drummed my fingers on the side of her hatch, "do you want to go grab a drink or something?"

She glanced at me, dimples gone.

"My treat," I amended.

"No, thanks." Stepping away, she pressed the button to close the hatch. I leaned back to keep from being hit.

"Saturday plans?" I asked.

"Nope." She dug through her satchel for keys.

I let out a breath as I ran my hand back through my hair. "I don't suppose next week—"

"Nope." She turned for the driver's seat.

"Rue. Samantha." I caught her wrist; she stopped, and I let go. I don't know why I cared so much—if a woman wasn't into me, she wasn't into me. But something about Rue intrigued me—sparked something in a part of me I thought had died. I would never forgive myself if I gave up without a fight. "Listen, give me a chance. I'll take you anywhere you want to go." Her countenance only seemed to fall with every offer. "Everything will be on me. You can set the terms—no touching, no *talking*, if that's what you want. I'll do all the driving—"

Her hand shot up between us. "Stop selling to me."

I choked on my words, instantly forgetting what I was about to say. "What?"

"Stop *selling* to me," she snapped. "I'm not one of your

goddamned customers." She pivoted on the toe of her boot and grabbed the handle of the driver-side door.

"I'm not . . . I'm not selling to you." I tried retracing my words. Was I?

She wrenched open the door. "Just go, Landry."

"Rue, I just—"

"*No.*" She whirled on me with all the force of a hurricane and stuck her unmanicured finger in my face. Her eyes beamed bright with anger—so bright I felt like she'd punched me. "I *waited* for you. I waited for you all freaking day at that stupid Ren faire, did you know that?"

Tears glistened above her eyelashes. I tried desperately to scrape something from my brain, *anything* to say, but I was at a loss.

"*You* asked *me*, remember?" she went on, volume increasing. "You wanted me to 'show you the ropes,' to get a costume together. I went and I waited for you and you *never* showed up and I got the worst damn sunburn of my life. And you didn't even *remember me!*"

Feeble words finally jumped the gap as my stomach sank into my hips. "Y-You looked different!"

She took a step forward. Instinctively, I backtracked, even as waves of rejection crashed into me. "I only look different because you forgot what I looked like! Did you even glance at those photos I sent more than once? Did you ever try to find me, to look me up on social media? There are hundreds of pictures on there. 'Looking different' is *not* an excuse."

Her cheeks were flushed. Not a single tear had fallen from her eyes, like they feared her wrath should they escape. A blessed wind passed by, cooling perspiration that beaded on my temples.

I was a complete imbecile.

"I'm sorry," I said, only half as loud as I'd intended. "You're right. I'm sorry."

Her gaze dashed between both my eyes before she threw her hands in the air. "What am I supposed to do with that, Landry?"

Rolling my lips together, I dared suggest, "You could accept it." God knew I would feel an iota better if she did.

She shook her head. "Yeah, I could."

But she didn't. She ducked into the cab of her SUV and slammed the door shut, driving away without further comment.

Super exited to go home! I can't beleive it's only three weeks away. It feels like Ive been here fifteen years and fifteen days at the same time. And that costume for the ren fair looks awsome, thanks! Is there a costume contest? We're totaly going to win it.

So exited to meet you, Sam. Here's my email. I bet you're ~~prettye~~ prettier in person than in your pics.

Chapter 8

IT STILL SUCKED two weeks later.

I know I talk big game, but I've been rejected before. TaLeah took the cake on that one, but I was well aware I wasn't everyone's cup of tea. But, to be cliché, there were so many fish in the sea. I always reminded myself of that. Usually keeping busy, hanging out with friends, and morning affirmations got me over a rejection quick. I actually kind of prided myself on how systematically I could move on.

But this time, it wasn't working.

It *bugged* me. Not the rejection itself. If I whittled that down to its purest form, it hurt, yeah, but it didn't *bug*. It was the rest of it. The way she'd stripped me down with a few select words until I was little more than a sunburned caveman left out in the middle of a desert. The way she'd dug up my faults—the ones I like to ignore—and then piled on new ones. *Those* are what nagged at me so badly.

I'd considered the Renaissance faire, briefly. Assured myself it hadn't been a big deal.

It had. And yeah, eight years had passed, but man, did that make me feel like an absolute tool.

And the *selling* thing. Rue had told me to stop selling to her. For the first few days, I'd fumed over that. What did she think I was? I wasn't *selling* anything. Sorry for liking you, guess that won't be a problem in the future (it still was).

But I couldn't stop thinking about it. Any place quiet settled in, it replayed in my mind. The elevator at work, driving in my car, staring at my ceiling as I tried to fall asleep at night.

And I think . . . I think she was right. I was selling to her. Not just in the parking lot either. LARPing, the singles mixer, the library . . . I was *selling* to her. In my words, a little, but definitely in my tone, my expression, and my thoughts. I knew the kind of smile people wanted to see. I knew the kind of responses they wanted to hear. I'd learned them from years of sales and sales training. And they'd ingrained themselves into me, become part of who I was. Ninety-nine percent of the time, it was fine. It worked. It was great.

And then I reconnected with the one percent, and everything fell apart. Because now, leaning against the cool glass of my living room window, staring out into Salt Lake City, I had to ask myself a question.

Who was I?

Moreover, who would I be if I hadn't gone into sales? If I'd become an accountant like my dad or gone into business instead or something else entirely? If I'd never done sales training and summer door-knocking and the whole affair . . . how different of a person would I be?

I was scared to examine the answer. I identified as *this* so well, but how much of *this* was, essentially, people pleasing?

I liked being liked. Everyone liked being liked, regardless

of what they claimed. No one truly craved negative attention. But if I could flip some switch in my brain, if I could truly *not care*—the way Rue seemed to—what would I evolve into?

Who was Landry Harrison, underneath it all?

I pressed the side of my fist against the glass and let out a long-held breath. I wanted to know the answer. I wanted to know how Rue did it.

Against all reason, all sanity, and all self-preservation, I wanted *Rue*.

She'd wanted me too, once. She'd waited for me at that Renaissance faire. She wouldn't be so angry if at least some small part of her didn't still care, right? I just had to figure out how to fan the embers back into a flame. Give it one more *sincere* shot, and if she still said no, I'd step away forever.

Shaking my head, I laughed at myself. Three nos. That was another sales tactic. You never accepted the first two.

And the funniest thing of all?

I weirdly missed LARPing.

RUE

I'd checked Business | Child Entrepreneurs | Lemonade Stands three times now.

Sighing, I leaned my chin into my palm and scrolled around my Excel sheet, not really reading anything. I was distracted today. I'd been distracted *a lot* lately, which was not doing any favors for my job performance. Leaning back, I pulled out my phone and opened Spotify, scrolling around to find a decent podcast to listen to. Unfortunately, I'd already listened to all the shows I liked. No new updates.

If you're going to waste time, you might as well waste it well.

Frowning, I clicked out of the library's software and opened up Facebook. Scrolled for a minute before checking my notifications. Clicked over to Herospect. Rhonda had posted a pair of reading glasses with the caption, *These belong to any of ours?*

Landry hadn't come to the last two sessions, which should have pleased me, but it just irked me in a different way. It was rude to leave Rhonda hanging to make the story work with a suddenly absent character. It was good that he was giving me space. It was stupid that I cared either way.

The pinned post in the group was for the potluck. Oh yeah. I clicked on the link to the Google doc and frowned when I saw all the dessert slots had been taken. I tapped my fingers on the mouse, considering. My mom made these bacon-tomato-cup things out of biscuit dough. Easy enough. Almost like a savory cupcake.

I scrolled up to type it in, then saw Landry's name. My body reacted like an electric current passed through it.

Landry Harrison – Lobster bisque

I rolled my eyes. Lobster bisque? Really? Who was he trying to impress?

Oh, right. Me.

I was tempted to delete the entry and write over it, but my adult senses forbade it and I wrote *Rue Thompson – Bacon-tomato things* beneath it. Moved my mouse to click out of the page, but my gaze slinked back to Landry's name.

Why does he even care? I am not *his type.* Still, rolling my lips together, I closed the doc and clicked over to the members section of the group, searching L-A-

Landry's profile link popped up. I clicked it.

His profile picture was of him posing in front of the big globe thing at Disney World. It looked to be a few years old. I clicked on it, then scrolled through his other photos. The next was him—and some friends—at a sushi place, nigiri pinched between chopsticks halfway to his mouth. The next was him with different friends at the beach. His hair was longer—dislike—and he was just in swim trunks. Dude definitely hit the gym. I clicked Next just to prove to myself that I didn't care if he was hot.

The next photo repeated that electric-shock feeling. My stomach squeezed halfway to inside out.

It was a picture of Landry on his mission, with a mission companion I didn't recognize. Not Wyatt. But he was in a suit and tie, standing in front of some Christmas light display, smiling at the camera. He was slimmer than he was now, his face a little leaner, younger. Jaw less prominent.

It affected me because this was the Landry I had known. Because he'd sent me this *exact* photo in one of his letters. I'd pull it out every now and then, along with some others, when I thought about him or when I wrote to him.

Biting the inside of my cheek, I clicked out of his profile pictures. Noticed our friend status—request pending. When had he sent me a friend request?

Ignoring it, I scrolled down and clicked on his photos.

Most of his pictures were him with people. Girls, guys, parents, kids. I could have uploaded any one of them to a Wikipedia article on extroverts. Most, I noticed, were posted by other people—Landry seemed to be one who used Facebook but didn't upload regularly. Like me.

I clicked through. So many of the women in the photos were fake-pretty—a term I'd coined for real-life people who looked like they were photoshopped but weren't. They just looked that way or were expert makeup artists who created the illusion of digital perfection on skin.

I clicked, clicked, clicked—paused. Clicked back.

Group photo outside what I guessed was a haunted house. It was dark outside, so someone had used the flash on their phone. It glimmered off a diamond ring on a girl's hand, which just happened to be pressed against Landry's chest as they smiled at the camera.

Engagement ring.

The conversation from my last family dinner surfaced. I hovered my mouse over the woman, but she wasn't tagged. Checked the comments—halfway down someone had said *You and Landry are perfect together!!* and a woman named TaLeah Poster had replied, *Thanks <3.*

I clicked on her profile.

It was a public profile, so I had full access to her friends list and photos. She wasn't Facebook friends with Landry, but if this woman was the ex-fiancée, that didn't surprise me. She was really pretty—fake-pretty in some pictures, naturally stunning in others. Tan (looked natural), long hair (definitely extensions), looked like she stepped out of a fashion magazine (or so I assumed; I never read them). I scrolled through her photos, but couldn't find any of her and Landry together. She must have deleted them. That one from the haunted house must have been uploaded by another friend.

"Not your kind of girl," I murmured to myself, clicking

out of Facebook and pulling up work again. From what I could venture from a curated social media profile, TaLeah Poster and I were polar opposites. Extrovert, introvert. Beach babe, library chick. Acrylic nails, untamed cuticles.

Then again, Elder Harrison and I had been very different, and past Rue, Samantha, had certainly had the hots for him.

Groaning, I rubbed my palms into my eyes. I wished I could flash forward a month or so to when I *stopped* thinking about this on a daily basis and got back to normal. I just wanted *normalcy*.

But I had a strange inkling I wasn't going to get it.

After a workday that felt way too long to be legal, I drove home, parked, and checked the mailbox, pulling out what belonged to my downstairs neighbors and leaving it at their doorstep for them to find. As I slipped inside my door, I noticed a Washington address on one of the letters.

Blaine!

Hurrying inside, I dropped the mail on the counter and tore open the card. As expected, it was a bridal shower invitation. Being thrown by a Melissa Baker, who I assumed was a friend of Blaine's mom. The invitation was stenciled with roses and had a little card for Blaine and Lysander's registry. Amazon was listed, which would make shipping them a package easier.

Licking my teeth, I looked at the date and, curious, checked my phone calendar. What if I *did* go? I had every intention of attending the wedding, which was six weeks later. Flying into Spokane twice seemed like overkill. But why not?

I had a ton of time off saved up, and I could use the break. Maybe if I got my body out of Utah, my brain would focus on something else—I'd just have to let Rhonda know I wouldn't make it this Saturday.

I was seriously considering it as I thumbed through the rest of the mail—junk, water bill, junk—and I found a letter addressed to me, handwritten, no return address. It was probably also junk mail—sometimes companies handwrote on the envelope to trick people into opening it. With a shrug, I tore the envelope open, finding a single piece of folded lined paper inside. Opening it up, I dropped my eyes to the signature.

It was a letter from Landry.

Chapter 9

Please don't throw this away.

I rolled my eyes, ignoring the hard pump of my heart, and read on.

First, I want to apollogize for selling to you.

His spelling still sucked, but it was a good enough start.

I didn't realize I was—admitedly, it's kind of engrained in me. That's not an excuse, just an explanation. I'm working on turning it off. Leaving work at work, you know? Never been something I was good at.

So I'm sorry for selling to you, and I really am genuinly sorry for ghosting you all those years ago.

I scoffed and marched toward the garbage can. Curiosity made me glance back.

> *Please don't throw this in the trash! Read until the end.*

I paused, one foot on the pedal that opened the trash can lid. A weird feeling washed over me, like I was on candid camera or something. That he knew me well enough, somehow, to know what I was going to do with this letter.

My pulse didn't let up.

I read on.

> *One last chance, Rue. This was how it all started, so I want to try again. No comitment from you. No "read" notification to give you away. Just a letter from me.*
>
> *(Please don't get mad at your brother for giving me your adress.)*

I snorted. Wyatt *would* pay; I'd just have to figure out in what manner I wanted to torture him.

> *So, hi. My name is Landry. Londry, if you prefer.*

Nerd.

> *I'm 29 years old, born and raised in Florida, recently moved to Utah for a job promotion. I live in Salt Lake City. Really different from*

home, but I'm enjoying it so far. My favorite
restarant is, wierdly, a vegan place down the
street, though I've always considered myself
a meat-eater.

I frowned at his grammar, all while fighting a press of déjà vu. *Weird* was a word he could *never* get right in his letters before. Still hadn't learned that it wasn't an I-before-E situation.

Where is your favorite place to eat? Favorite
food? Have you ever lived out of state? If you
had to move, where would you go? Anywhere
in the world is free game.
  It's nice to meet you, Rue.
  Sincerely,
  Landry H.

I set the letter on the counter. Folded my arms and stared at it. *Why, Landry? Why now?*

I hated the way my heart drummed. I hated the neat slant to his cursive. I hated the effort and the niceness.

The letter sat on the counter through dinner and a brief Netflix binge.

It made its way into the trash before I turned in for the night.

I ordered plane tickets on my lunch break the next day. Decided not to call Blaine—let it be a surprise. I did RSVP to Melissa, though. I was a stickler for RSVPing, thanks to my party-crazed mother and her party-crazed party-rule-following. After work, I swung by Target, printed out Blaine's registry, and got her a set of rainbow mixing bowls, plus some Sour Punch Straws and a set of unicorn-themed measuring cups that weren't on her list. I brought my purchases home and checked the mail.

There was an ad from the local grocery store and a letter addressed to me, this time with a return address in Salt Lake City, but no name. Still, I recognized the handwriting. Still, my heart kicked into gear, making me feel like I'd just finished a derby game.

Inside, I set the letter on the counter and stared at it, waiting for Superman lasers to come out of my eyes. They didn't. I heated up leftovers. Ate while I stared at the letter. Set my dishes in the sink. Opened it.

> *Hey Rue,*
>
> *How was work today? What exactly do you do at the library besides help illegal county aleins find books?*

I couldn't help but smile at that.

> *I drove up the canyon today. We don't have canyons in Florida—they still blow my mind, despite having lived here before. The size of the mountains, the expanse of the trees . . . how long did it take to make those roads?? Incredeble. I can't wait for fall. I love driving through the mountains when the leaves are changing.*

I liked driving through the canyons during fall too. Not that I said as much. Not that he would have heard me if I had.

What's your favorite season? You may have told me before. You seem like an autum person. Summer too hot—sunburns. Winter is too cold, too dreary. Not enough color. Spring is always nice, but it rains all the time, and Utah springs can't decide if they want to be summer or winter. Like they don't have an identity of their own.

> *Did I get it right?*

I chewed on my lip. He had.

You probably guessed that I'm a summer guy.

Indeed.

I'm performing at the Club on 6th this week-end. Comedy, ha. I'm nervous, but I'm always nervous. I don't do this enough to not be nervous. I want to tell you to stop by, but it's always worse when I know someone in the ~~adience~~ *audience. So . . . there's that. Maybe I shouldn't have said anything.*

> *Hope your day is going well and your air conditioner works.*
> *Sincerely,*
> *Landry H.*

I left the letter on the counter and went to craft some earrings out of my bead kit, start a load of laundry, and pick up my bedroom. Before heading to bed, I snatched it off the counter and headed toward the garbage. Paused.

And shoved it in the kitchen drawer where I kept my bills.

Another letter came Wednesday, two pages long.

> *We're hiring this week. Interviews are so strange to me. The livlihoods of all these people are in my hands. And even if we do two or three rounds, I'm still hiring technical strangers. They could be God's gift to the company or an absolute reck.*
>
> *If you could do anything, magically snap you fingers and have all the ~~critiria~~ criteria needed, what would it be? Once I would have said a standup comic, but I don't think so anymore. I actually think it'd be interesting to work in a zoo.*

When I came home Thursday, I found myself heading toward the mailbox before my car could fully settle into park. I didn't examine the excitement or anything else. I didn't want to. I just wanted to see if it would be there.

It was. Another letter. This one a single page.

I opened it right there on the side of the road.

I really hate broccoli.

"No salutation?" I asked, and continued reading.

> *I feel guilty about it. Isn't that stupid? I eat plenty of other vegetables. But broccolli seems like THE quissential vegetable.*

No, carrots were.

> *It's not even the taste. It just recks my system. I'm going to leave it at that because I don't even know if you're reading this, and if you suddenly decide to start on this one . . . well, I don't think I'm going to charm you with stories of my enthusiastic ~~bowls~~ bowels.*

Smiling, I walked into the house, not bothering to scoop out the rest of the mail. The other tenants could grab it. I sat at the counter—it was a brief letter. Landry was likely running out of stuff to say, given he had nothing to respond to.

I finished the letter. Read it again from the top.

This is how he got you the first time, my sour little inner voice said in the back of my head. *It's easier to put on an act on paper than in person.*

Maybe it was, for some people. I considered myself a decent writer—I could feign my identity in a letter better than I could on a stage, though then again, LARPing gave me plenty of practice pretending to be someone else.

LARPing had also shown me that Landry struggled to do just that. Maybe it was only the fantasy aspect of it or the costumes, but he kind of sucked at getting into character.

Stepping around the counter, I opened the drawer with his other letters, thinking to reread the first—the original olive branch—only to remember I'd thrown it away, and garbage day had come and passed. Regret prickled my insides, but there was nothing I could do about it now.

Folding the newest letter up, I dropped it in the drawer. Stared at the three I'd collected.

Then I strode into the second bedroom, where my home office was, and grabbed a fresh piece of paper. I sat down right there, grabbed a purple gel pen, and wrote,

> *Landry,*
> *No one likes broccoli. Except sociopaths.*
> *So there's one thing going for you.*
> *If I could have any job in the world, I would be a food critic exclusively for bakeries.*
> *I'd probably live in Canada.*
> *Rue*

I hesitated a moment, looking over my brief note and my messy handwriting. Nerves tied together in my gut, making me feel a little nauseous.

Before I could second-guess myself, I shoved the letter in an envelope, addressed it, and stuck it in the mailbox.

I wasn't going to come. I genuinely had no intention to.

But I had to drive north for the airport anyway, which wasn't too far from Club on 6th, so . . .

I arrived after the show had started. There was a lineup of several performers, but Landry was second, according to the poster outside, and he'd already started when I slipped inside after showing my ID and getting my hand stamped. It was fortunately dark inside, and a lot of the stage lighting was red for . . . night vision? I don't know. Despite the darkness, I didn't take any of the available chairs. Just hovered in the back. I wasn't planning on staying long. I was just curious.

Just curious. Felt like I'd been using that excuse a lot lately.

"Let's hear another one," Landry said, crossing the stage. He wore dress pants with a business-casual button-up, the top two buttons undone, no tie, sleeves rolled up just below his elbows. His hair looked newly cut. Handsome as ever. My ensuing frown had become a reflex.

He pointed to someone in the audience.

"Cheetahs," the woman said.

"Cheetahs. Yep, pretty standard," he replied before pointing at someone else. "You?"

"Eagles."

"It's always carnivores, isn't it?" he asked, getting a couple of chuckles. Someone near the back raised their hand; I pressed into the wall, trying to be invisible, which I realized was slightly harder with freshly redyed pink hair. But Landry didn't notice me. Probably struggled to see past the stage lights, period.

"Beetdiggers!" the man in the back yelled.

The room laughed, and I realized he'd asked them for high school mascots. Beetdiggers was one of the weirder local ones.

After the giggling calmed down, Landry nodded and said, "Technically still a carnivore. Or a very dangerous omnivore."

I fought against a smile.

"Now." He moved back to center stage and bent forward like he was getting ready for a big reveal. "If any of you plan on founding a school, I'm about to make it the *best* school ever. No matter what competition your students are in—debate, football, cheer, band—they will have the ultimate mascot. That's right. I am going to tell you the *ultimate mascot*, the one that will defeat any opponent—cheetah, eagle, even beetdigger."

A few chuckles sounded through the room.

He stared into the audience, silent. Purposely letting an awkward amount of time pass, earning another couple chuckles. Then, the microphone pressed close to his lips, he asked in a deep voice, "Are you ready?"

I rolled my eyes, but a clipped laugh wiggled up my throat.

"To meet," he continued. Paused. Scanned the audience. "The Tallahassee Tapeworms!"

I snorted. The audience was a mixture of laughs and groans. Landry waved his hands as though trying to calm them down.

"Hear me out, hear me out," he said. "*Think* about it! Cheetah vs. Tapeworm. Who wins? Tapeworm."

He had a point.

"Eagle vs. Tapeworm. Who wins? Tapeworm."

Someone in the front row clearly thought this was the funniest thing she'd ever heard, she was laughing so hard.

"Beetdigger vs. Tapeworm. Who wins?"

The audience recited, "Tapeworm!"

Landry clapped his hands in victory, creating a loud *thunk* through the speakers. "Imagine football games! A big flesh-colored mascot with poles, like those Chinese dragons, marching up and down the track."

He mimed holding a pole and marching across the stage. I tried not to laugh, but it escaped my mouth anyway.

"Be aggressive! B-E aggressive!" he recited the popular cheer. "Be digestive! B-E digestive!"

Grinning, I checked my watch. I both did and didn't want to stay. Fortunately, the airline made the choice for me.

Keeping close to the wall, I escorted myself out and headed to the airport.

Chapter 10

I HELD MY gift in front of my face when the door opened, letting two others—both in oversize gift bags—hang off my arms.

"Hello!" said an unsure, unfamiliar voice.

I peeked around my present at a stranger's face. "Hi! Are you Melissa?"

She lit up. "Yes! And you are?" She stepped aside to let me in.

"A surprise," I whispered, and quickly caught sight of Blaine on a white sofa in the front room, chatting with another woman I didn't recognize. Let's be honest—I wasn't going to recognize *anyone* here. I dug deep, deep down into my soul for my extrovert panties and pulled them on.

They pinched.

Keeping my gift in front of my face, I shuffled over to Blaine. Couldn't see her face, but I watched her knees shift as she turned toward me. "Hi!" she said. "Who—"

I shoved the gift into her lap and posed with the two gift bags. "Ta-da."

"OH MY GOSH!" She sprung off the couch, forcing my present to the floor—that was okay, it wasn't fragile—and leapt at me, then closed her arms around my shoulders. She jumped, making the hug exciting and awkward, but I was super relieved that she was, actually, happy to see me. "RUE, YOU CAME, YOU VIXEN LIAR."

"I didn't lie!" I laughed, managing to shift the gift backs to hug her back.

"Omitting the truth is lying!" Blaine pulled back, grinning ear to ear.

"We are *not* having this argument again." Omitting the truth was *not* lying, and I had a full soapbox case for it that Blaine had heard multiple times.

She wiped a finger under her eye, which made my little black heart swell three sizes, just like my cousin the Grinch. "You didn't have to fly all this way! I feel bad!" She hugged me again.

"I needed a vacation." I squeezed her and pulled back, handing her the bags that were starting to dig into my elbows. "These are from the derby girls."

"Oh, that's so nice! I miss them." She took the bags and looked over them like they were priceless jewels.

Melissa, smiling, stepped over and said, "Here, I'll take these."

"Thank you." Blaine handed them over, along with my wrapped box, then sat on the couch and pulled me down beside her. "Kanisha, I'm so sorry," she addressed the woman she'd been speaking to when I arrived. "This is Rue, one of my best friends from Utah. She was in derby with me."

Kanisha waved. "Nice to meet you!" Patting Blaine's

knee, she said, "There's a chicken salad sandwich calling my name, so you two catch up."

"Ooh, chicken salad." I looked over toward the food table, ogling the spread. "Oh man, I forget parties like this are way better outside of Utah." Seriously, though. It was a weird cultural thing to make everything an open house with brownies, lemonade, and nothing else.

Blaine swatted me. "It's not . . . *always* that bad." She laughed.

I pointed to a lock of violet hair falling over her shoulder. "What is *this*?" I snatched it. Blaine's peekaboo had been electric blue for as long as I'd known her.

She shook her head like she starred in an Herbal Essences ad. "I let my mom choose the color. You like?"

"I do." I preferred electric blue, but violet wasn't *bad*. "Maybe I'll dye mine to match."

"Ha! You should."

I wiggled my hands. "Lemme see it."

It took half a second for Blaine to catch on before she thrust her left hand forward. "What do you think?"

"Ooh, no one goes for yellow gold anymore," I said, admiring the ring. It had three emerald-cut diamonds on it, the center being the largest. I turned her hand over and paused. "Is this . . . is this the one ring?" There was finely engraved Tengwar script—yep, from The Lord of the Rings—on the band.

Blaine grinned. "Most people don't notice. It was Lysander's idea."

"Of course it was Lysander's idea. Nerd."

She cocked an eyebrow, and I knew exactly what she didn't say. *You of all people, calling another a nerd?*

But I was so good at it.

Others shortly came into the room—I abandoned Blaine for food while she greeted other guests, and returned to play a game Melissa had put together, which involved us taking off our shoes and poking socks on the floor with our feet. Each sock had some sort of honeymoon "necessity" in it, and we had to guess what it was. Of course, there were giggles for the condom and lube, but there was also ChapStick, Kleenex, deodorant, lotion, and graciously, a hundred-dollar bill.

"This is so nice," Blaine said as the scores were tallied and the items gifted to her. "Thank you!"

I came in second, so I just missed winning the prize, which was a gift card to a local coffee shop I wouldn't have been able to use anyway.

"Did everyone fill out an index card?" Melissa asked, and she gestured to a table I hadn't seen by the door with a guest book and a stack of colorful three-by-fives. I got up and walked over to it—they were pieces of advice for Blaine and Lysander. I was hardly one to give advice on relationships, let alone marriage, but I picked up a pink card and a pen and started writing.

Always go to bed angry. I'd heard that one a couple times. Then I added, *And in something slutty.*

I paused after signing my name. The act brought Landry to mind unbidden.

Had he written me a letter yesterday? Today? How long would he keep it up before it got too tiring? Did he receive mine? What did he think?

Sighing, I stuffed my advice card into the awaiting box. I came to Washington to *not* think about Landry. Still, I itched to know. Would it be weird to call my downstairs neighbor and ask her to check? Or have her read it to me over the phone?

Reading over the phone would be weird. We didn't really know each other. And what if Landry wrote something personal?

Did I want him to write something personal? Moreover, did I want to *admit* that I wanted him to keep writing me?

No, I didn't.

"Have you done," said a twenty-something whose name I couldn't remember as I returned, "the thirty-six questions thing?"

"Thirty-six questions?" Blaine asked.

"Oh, I know that," Kanisha said. "It's this neuroscience something where you ask a stranger thirty-six questions—specific ones—and then you stare into their eyes for four minutes."

"I've actually heard of it," I said without really thinking as I sank down next to Blaine. I mean, I kind of knew it. Courtney had been talking about it in the car on the way to Salt Licks for that dating thing.

Which instantly brought Landry back to mind. My hormones relived the mortification of seeing him again all on their own, and it made me squelchy.

"Huh, no." Blaine considered. "Four minutes is a long time."

"I know!" said the twenty-something. "You can watch people do it on YouTube, and even clipped, it seems like forever. But it also seems to work?"

"She doesn't need it," said Lisa, Blaine's mom. Her health

seemed to be much improved, though I'd never seen her in person before today. "She's already got the nail in the coffin."

The women chuckled at that.

I glanced to the twenty-something. "What kind of questions?"

"Um." She thought for a minute, then pulled out her phone. Clicked around. "What is your most treasured memory?" she read from the screen. "For what in your life do you feel the most grateful? When did you last sing to yourself?"

"Huh," I said.

"Those aren't what I was expecting," Blaine added. "Can I see?"

The gal handed over her phone. I started to read over Blaine's shoulder, but the text was tiny, and the front door opened, distracting me.

"Oh hi!" Lisa called. I looked over to see a *familiar* face for once. Lysander walked in holding about eighteen grocery bags.

"Got any eggs?" I asked, and Blaine laughed.

Inside joke.

Blaine handed the phone back and stood. "Let me help you!"

Lysander flushed. "S-Sorry, I was going to sneak in the garage, but the code wasn't working."

"It's fine!" Blaine assured him, unloading several bags. I hurried over as well, followed by Kanisha, and we each took a handful of handles and carried them into the pantry. Lysander apologized again, and we all reassured him.

Listen, I'm an introvert. But I'm like Carrot Top compared to Lysander.

He was looking good, healthy, all that jazz. I knew he had moved in with Blaine and her mom recently—they'd both stay at the house until Blaine's mom's health was solidly stable, which would, with luck, be soon. Even then, I don't know if they'd move far. Blaine wasn't very close to her dad, and she tended to worry.

Lysander made himself scarce after that. We opened gifts— yes, the derby crowd purchased Blaine many scandalous things, so it was probably a good thing Lysander hadn't stayed. Things wound down after that. I was the last to pack up, but before I could say my goodbyes, Blaine seized my wrist and asked, "Are you staying in a hotel?"

I rolled my eyes. "No, I'm sleeping at the McDonald's down the street."

"Cancel your room. You should stay here!"

I smiled. "It's only for one night. All my stuff is there. And I think it's a little late to cancel."

Blaine mulled over that for a moment. "Don't move." She spun on her heel, skirt flying, and hurried down the stairs. She took several minutes, so I made myself comfortable on the couch and pulled out my phone. Found myself wandering to Facebook. Landry's friend request was sitting there in my notifications.

I might have given in, clicked on it, if Blaine hadn't rushed back into the living room. Instead, I tucked my phone away, leaving the notification untouched. She had her old derby duffel bag over one shoulder.

"Okay, I'm sleeping over."

I snorted. "What?"

"Let's go!" She marched to the door. "Ly will hold the fort here. We're catching up. I'll drive."

"This is so fancy," Blaine said as I pushed open the door to the chain hotel I'd gotten a room in.

"The fanciest," I retorted. "They even put sheets on the bed."

Blaine bounced onto the queen mattress. "Clean ones?"

I snorted. "I'm not made of cash. I just sleep on the comforter." I gestured to the far end. "You can sleep there. I like being close to the bathroom." I dropped my purse on a chair, then plopped down beside it. "Blaine."

"Hm?"

"You're getting *married!*" It was weird—I knew she was getting married. I'd known for a while. But for some reason, right then, it hit me. "*Blaine May.* Has a nice ring to it." I paused. "Are you changing your name?"

"I should probably make up my mind on that, eh? *Lysander Wickers* is sort of a mouthful." She ran her hand over a fluffed pillow—housekeeping had been by while I was away. "I like the idea of sharing a last name. It makes it so official. But it's a pain in the butt to change all the documentation and such. And then there's hyphenating, but that seems a little extreme. Except his is only one syllable, so it's not that big of a deal. But isn't it annoying to hyphenate someone's name all the time? People default to the last-last one, anyway."

"Blaine Wickers-May." I considered. "Not too bad. But yeah, you're running out of time to decide."

Blaine smiled. Picked up the pillow and chucked it at me. "You're not changing yours anytime soon, are you?"

I punched down the pillow in my lap and leaned my elbows onto it. "Please."

"Nothing new?"

"No." I curled my toes in my shoes. "Not . . . really."

Her eyes narrowed at me. "That is the most Rue way of saying yes that I know."

I rolled my eyes. "It's just awkward."

"Tell me!" She bounced on the bed, ever full of energy. Patted the mattress beside her.

I chucked the pillow at her. "Really though, it's awkward. Don't get excited."

She did her best to sober her expression. "Okay. I'm ready."

"Do you remember . . ." My insides squirmed, but if I could tell anyone, it was Blaine. And she was apart from all of it, which meant no mess. Not that Blaine would gossip about it anyway, but it was an added measure of security. "The missionary I wrote to, who ghosted me? Who ran into me a while back?"

Blaine's eyebrows popped with surprise. "Yes . . . is there more to that story?"

I sighed. "So I actually first ran into him at this dumb singles mixer Wyatt made me go to. And he didn't remember who I was." My phone buzzed. I checked the screen—it was from Cameron, sending me some random GIF. He didn't text me very often; we usually only talked at LARP or on Facebook about LARP. I set the phone aside.

Blaine blanched. "Is that him?"

"No."

Studying me, she asked, "How long did you write him, again?"

"A little over a year."

"Jerk."

"Right?" I held out my hand for that pillow—I liked the support of it. Blaine chucked it across the room, and I stuck it under my elbows. "He realized it later, and he looked like a doofus, and it was great."

"I want details."

I shook my head. "That's not the thing, though. He started LARPing with my group."

"Really?"

I nodded. "Yeah. He asked me out twice—"

Blaine's mouth formed a long O.

"—and I told him no both times."

Her mouth closed.

"The second time I kind of . . . yelled at him a little? But now he's writing me letters, trying to start again the way we did in the beginning."

She scoffed. "Dude needs to take a hint!"

"Yeah," I said half-heartedly.

I could feel Blaine's eyes on me as I stared at the colored speckles in the hotel carpet. "You want him to take a hint . . . yes?"

I shrugged. "I guess so."

"That's the most Rue way of saying no I've ever heard."

I twisted my mouth. "I don't really know what I want."

"Do you like him?"

I almost threw the pillow at her again. "If I knew that, I wouldn't be struggling!"

"Okay, okay." She put up her hands in surrender. "Do you think about him a lot?"

I didn't want to answer that.

But Blaine knew me well. "Good thinking or bad thinking?"

"Both," I admitted.

She pressed a knuckle to her chin. "Hmm."

"Hmm," I repeated.

"It's just," she said, measuring her words, "you're not interested in a whole lot of people. I've seen you date one person seriously the entire time I've known you, and even that wasn't for very long."

I shrugged. "There's not a whole lot of people around Utah to be interested in." I'd thought of moving out of Utah several times, but all my family and friends were there, and I was comfortable there. Anytime I seriously looked into it, the wind fell out of my sails pretty quickly.

"There are a lot of interesting people everywhere," Blaine countered, "but someone has to be really interesting to catch your attention."

"But he's not even interesting," I protested. "He's a salesman. Like a walk-into-the-toy-store-and-pick-Ken-off-the-wall kind of guy."

"So he looks like Ken?"

I felt my face heat, which only pissed me off. "No. I mean, I guess he kind of does."

Blaine smirked. "Ken's hot."

"It's more than being hot."

"I'm well aware." Her tone remained measured. "What else?"

I frowned. "He's a super by-the-book Hallmark romance hero. It's annoying."

"So annoying. That's why those movies do so poorly," she teased.

"I saw, like, three minutes of his comedy show," I offered, staring down the carpet again. "He was decent."

"He's a comedian?"

"Amateur."

"Aren't we all, though." She pushed herself back on the mattress and drew her legs under her. See, I never wore skirts because of that. They limited how you could sit. I wanted freedom to sprawl my legs wherever I wanted.

"I never really told you," I tried, softer, "how much it sucked. I only mentioned it because of all your bad dating stories."

Blaine rolled her eyes. She really did have some horrific ones in her repertoire.

"But it *sucked* when he didn't show." The words trailed into a whisper, but I forced them out anyway. "We had plans. Or I thought we did. And I waited for him, and he never came." My throat got tight, and I cough-growled to loosen it up. "I . . . really liked him, Blaine. *Really* liked him. He felt like my lighthouse. He was so enthusiastic about my weird hobbies. So kind. So funny. So accepting. I invited him to a Renaissance faire. I made our costumes and waited outside the gates all day, only to be ghosted. Then, and forever, until this summer. It *sucked*. I will always hate him for that."

I had to.

We sat in silence for a minute before Blaine tentatively said, "That does suck. I can't imagine."

I chuckled. "You probably can."

Now she shrugged. "Can I pose a scenario for you?"

Warily, I nodded.

"What if *before* never happened?"

I put my heels on the edge of the chair and buried my chin into the pillow. "What do you mean?"

"What if you just happened to meet him at the . . . what

was it? A mixer? What if you just met him at the mixer, clean slate, and he was interested in you. What would you think?"

I mulled over it for half a second. "I'd think he was crazy."

"Why?"

My gut squirmed. I dug around for the most truthful answer I felt able to give. "Because guys like Landry don't go for girls like me."

"Ah, we have a name."

I threw up some sarcastic jazz hands.

"But he does, because he's chasing you," Blaine pressed. "Have you ever been chased before?"

I sank farther into the pillow. "No?" Unless you counted Cameron, but he didn't really *chase* me, and I certainly did not want to get caught. I'd told him that outright about six months after he joined Herospect. Now he just awkwardly appeared at random times, tried to convince me not to drive my car, and stole my keys.

"That's the thing about it, though," she went on. "When you want it, it's charming. When you don't want it, it's creepy. So which is it?"

I pushed my knees up so the pillow hid my entire face. As far as my awareness went, it was just me alone in a tight, downy room.

Which was it?

I wanted another letter. I knew that much. But I couldn't want it. I wasn't *supposed* to want it. Because wanting it went against everything I believed in. Every hurt, every outburst, every wall.

Didn't it?

"Want to go out for dinner?" Blaine asked after several minutes.

I nodded into the pillow.

"Okay." I heard her stand and dig through her duffel bag. "I know a great place nearby. My treat."

I lowered the pillow. "That's why you're my favorite."

She winked at me. "I know the way to your heart, Rue Thompson."

But I worried she wasn't the only one.

Chapter 11

I DELAYED MY flight a day to spend Sunday with Blaine and Lysander. I didn't know Lysander super well, but he was a pretty cool dude with a good head on his shoulders, and he looked at Blaine like she was the sun to his world. It made me really happy for them, but also a little sad for myself.

Monday morning I flew to Portland to visit a friend from college, and we spent two days hanging out at the coast and shopping at a million little boutiques. I didn't fly back to Utah until Wednesday evening.

Admittedly, as soon as I pulled into the driveway, I went straight to the mailbox. I hated the way disappointment filled my chest when there was nothing there.

Grabbing my carry-on from my car, I went inside and trekked straight to the counter, but my neighbors hadn't left mail there either. Did I get *nothing* the last five days?

Did he ghost me *again*?

Don't be stupid, I thought as I chucked my bag onto the couch. *He has a life. Maybe it was just a week-long experiment.*

But I'd replied to him! The bastard. And what did I care anyway? I didn't owe Landry Harrison anything—

Turning, I spied a stack of mail underneath the door at the top of the stairs, the ones that led into the basement apartment. *Stack* was a poor term—it looked like my neighbors had been just shoving my letters under the door. It was more of a scattered pile.

Still, my stupid heart lodged into my throat as I knelt to collect them. Finding one, two, three . . . *four* letters from Landry.

I left the rest on the floor and sat on the couch, organizing the envelopes by postdate to make sure I'd read them in order.

I tore open the first one, ripping part of the paper inside when I did.

> *Rue,*
>
> *I think Canada is the honist answer for most people. Change is hard, and Canada is the closest we have to the United States. Honestly, I'd probably do Canada too . . . except that it's cold. I hate the cold. Not looking forward to winter here.*
>
> *I am utterly relieved to know I'm not a sociopath. I feel like I can finally dispose of the bodys in my basement with a clear conscious.*

I snorted and rolled my eyes.

> *I never even THOUGHT of food critic! That would be an amazing job. Do you have a favorite bakery? Do you like patiserie? But*

of coarse you do. Only sociopaths don't like patiserie.

I did like patisserie and agreed with him on that.

So, you're technically a librarian. Or a super-librarian? I don't know how the ecosystem of that works (feel free to explain it to me). But what's your favorite thing to read? ~~Gener~~ Genre, title, author?

I don't tell a lot of people this (I don't know why. Maybe it never comes up, or no one is ever familier with the works), but I actually really like old-school science fiction. Things like Brave New World *and Lovecraft.*

That actually surprised me. And kind of impressed me. I finished the letter and moved on to the next.

Rue,

I don't mean to talk about myself, but today was terrible and I want to vent to someone.

He went into a laundry list of stuff that had gone wrong, like cells being installed upside down on a large project, manufacturing problems, and the COO of the company suddenly quitting. Then he got a flat tire on the way home and realized he'd forgotten to put an entire pork shoulder in the fridge after grocery shopping the night before.

I felt for him.

I hope your day went better than mine.

It had. That was Monday, when I flew into Portland.

I opened his third letter, getting a stupid tingly sensation when I read the heading.

Samantha Ruth Thompson,

I was really surprised he remembered my full name. And that he spelled it correctly.

I read down, looking over more questions about myself, then a spiel on color theory from an article he'd read. I read slower near the end.

> *I honestly didn't expect you to reply at all, so the one you sent was . . . good. But I can (kind of?) take a hint, so if these bother you, just let me know. I really will stop. All of it. No letters, no larping. I'll even part ways with Wyatt, if that makes you comfortable. Promise.*
> *You can text me if that's easier.*

He left his phone number.

My stomach twisted. He meant it—he would cut off all connections if I willed it, even if it meant dropping probably one of the only friends he had in the state. He might have worried because I hadn't sent him any other replies, which meant he didn't know I'd left town. I hadn't told him, of course, but that also meant he hadn't inquired to Wyatt about me . . . which I honestly appreciated. This was between Landry and me. No other players necessary.

I opened his last letter, frowning at its brevity.

> *Rue,*
>
> *How are you? Hair still pink? You know, pink was my favorite color growing up, but I was so afraid of being made fun of that I changed it to green. It was all a lie.*
>
> *Also, I was in love with Kimberly, the pink Power Ranger, for about three years. Maybe I still am. #celebritycrush.*

Nerd.

> *Okay. So. It was 100% my entent to woo you slowly. You know, write to you like I used to, maybe get the nerve to ask you to spend some time with me around Christmas if you hadn't completely ~~denow~~ denounced me. But. I saw in my newsfeed that Springville is hosting a small Renaisance fair.*

My gut sickened suddenly. I pinched the letter between my fingers.

> *I know you like Renaisance fairs, and there definitely aren't any in the winter (I checked). And . . . I'd like a redo. So I'm going to go. And I'd love you to go with me. To show me the ropes. For real this time. If and only if you want to. And I totally understand if you don't want to. I'm heading up Saturday.*

Afternoon, since I know you wouldn't want to miss larp.

In case you lost it, here's my number again, and you can text or call and tell me to get lost. Otherwise I'm heading to the Goodwill to piece together a costume that you'll probably hate.

Thanks for giving me a chance.

Landry

The rest of the letter was the address of the faire. Pinching my lips together, I googled it. This weekend. Looked like it was the first time the city was doing it. Definitely wasn't as big as the Ogden festival, but . . .

But this was my chance to get back at him.

The thought both thrilled and nauseated me.

I set the letter aside and rubbed warmth into hands suddenly gone cold. Left the letters on the couch and walked into my bedroom. Turned on the TV, but I didn't really want to watch anything. I left it on some reality show I'd never heard of and got into the shower and just . . . sat under the hot water, not really thinking of anything, yet somehow thinking of everything.

By the time I got out, I'd ruined the fashion color in my hair, and I went to bed on brassy, wet curls.

Thursday and Friday I worked overtime—despite not getting paid for it—just to keep my brain busy. Not because I had work to make up from my trip; no one was in a rush when it came to the Library of Congress, nor the government in general. I got home late and purposely did not check the mailbox, though both days, around sunset, one of my downstairs neighbors knocked on the door and handed me my letters. And Landry wrote me one for each day. Well, Thursday's was a postcard with a photo of Arches National Park featured on it.

Have you been here yet? the caption read.

That was it, but it snicked in my chest anyway. Been here *yet*. Because, despite being utterly able to recognize me even with Wyatt right there as a spotlight, Landry remembered that, at the age of twenty, I had not yet been to *any* of Utah's national parks, despite having been born and raised here.

I still hadn't. I'd also never gone skiing.

Friday's letter covered some of the cleanup of that terrible day earlier that week, ideas he had for LARPing if he ever played Londry again (still the worst character name ever), and a subtle reminder about the Renaissance faire tomorrow. He didn't reintroduce his phone number, just left it on the bottom of the page. In case I somehow didn't see it the last two times.

Friday night I drove to the local beauty supply store and dyed my hair blue. I still preferred pink, but Landry liked pink, so I chose blue. I *needed* to choose blue. I'd joked to Blaine about going violet, but violet had too much pink in it. So blue it was.

It didn't look too bad.

Saturday morning, before LARP, I looked up the Springville Renaissance Faire. It opened at 10:00 a.m. and went until 9:00 p.m. That's how I knew it wasn't a *true* Ren faire. Those went to at least midnight.

I made it to the park for Herospect early, eager to get my mind on something else.

Adelaide had a house showing at noon (she was a real estate agent), so we finished a little earlier, which saw me back home and making ramen noodles (*not* the cheap kind, thank you) by a quarter after twelve. Though my stomach was tight enough that I wasn't sure how kindly it would take to food.

Still, I'd made my decision. I was going to sit at home the rest of the day and binge-watch a new Korean drama. And Landry was going to sit at the park waiting for me and relive a portion of what I'd experienced. A portion, because Landry was not as invested in this as I had been eight years ago. Surely he wasn't *that* invested. But it would be satisfying enough.

I plopped on the couch with my noodles around 12:45 p.m. Started the show, but my focus kept drifting away from the subtitles. My ramen dried up in my mouth. My stomach hurt.

Stop it, I chided myself. *This is karma. This is how the universe rights itself.*

I started the episode over, but my thoughts kept drifting away, and my gaze flicked to and from the digital clock on the microwave: 1:01.

If I'd had this opportunity even a few months ago, I would be reveling in it. So why wasn't I reveling in it?

"*Stop,*" I whined to myself, setting my ramen aside. I strode into the kitchen, opened the drawer with Landry's letters, and threw them in the garbage. Returned to the couch. Pressed play.

I watched for about five minutes before my body started squirming of its own accord. Pausing the show, I dropped my head into my hands and took several deep breaths.

Was this the kind of person I wanted to be?

Hadn't Landry . . . changed? Or was, at the very least, trying to?

You like him.

"No, I don't," I said aloud, surprised at the tightness in my voice. I swallowed against my squeezing throat and tangled my fingers in my hair. "I don't. I don't. *I don't.*"

I can't.

Because if I liked Landry Harrison, I was betraying myself. I was stabbing Samantha in the back and spitting on her hurt. I was mocking her and her heartbreak. I would literally be insane, doing the same thing twice and expecting a different result.

Right?

I closed my eyes, and unbidden, my brain whirled back to old fantasies. Landry picking me up in his car, Landry with his arm around my shoulders on the couch, Landry with his hand in mine as we walked through Christmas lights at Temple Square. All stupid expectations I'd built up for myself from those hope-crested letters. All expectations that had shattered.

Except now Landry was older. More experienced, more mature. Now I could hear his voice, almost like those thoughts were memories, not fantasies. I could see the quirks in the way he moved, the way he smiled, the way he looked at me—things I couldn't quite piece together from letters and photos alone. And my heart hurt with each one.

What if I went and he wasn't there?

What if he left me behind again?

Why the hell was I crying?

I wiped a tear from my eye and went to the bathroom to splash cold water on my face. Scrubbed a little too hard with the hand towel and looked at myself in the mirror, temporarily startled because I wasn't used to the blue curls. I thought of Blaine up in the Palouse. She'd put herself out there again and again. She had a legitimate horror story to accompany each and every effort, even the one that ultimately worked out. But it *had* worked out for her, and she was happy. Happy, because she'd had the courage to risk her heart again and again and again.

Surely I could risk mine one more time.

Letting out a deep breath, I stared hard into the reflection of my eyes. "I'm sorry, Sam," I whispered. "I'm sorry. I thought I was over him, but I'm not. He's not even my type, but"—I swallowed—"I like Landry."

Squeezing the edges of the sink, I continued, "But I remember how it felt. I really do. So . . . this is stupid, but I need your permission to go. I need to know it's okay to go."

I stared at the sink plug for a solid minute before glancing up at myself again. And, for a minute, I saw myself as I had been, before I'd cut off my hair and changed its color, before I got jaded by the world and consoled myself with my own rage.

I saw Samantha, and she smiled at me.

LANDRY

This might have been a fool's errand, but I didn't want to live with the regret of not trying. I had plenty of other things to regret without adding a possible second chance with Rue to the list.

So I pulled up to the park where the festival was happening. It wasn't walled in or anything, but there was a big flower arch at the entrance where you paid for tickets and scanned a QR code for a map that included both the history of Renaissance faires and the history of Springville City. I'd scanned it already and scrolled through while leaning against the hood of my Tesla, waiting. One person came out early on and asked if I was supposed to be working the weaver's booth, probably because I was the only guest I'd seen in costume. A costume that consisted of an oversize dress shirt, a vest from the sixties, and brown slacks I'd cut just below the knee. I'd used shoelaces to tie the cut leg in place, and I'd bought women's knee-high stockings at the store. They didn't come in many colors—the most Renaissance-y ones I could find were navy.

I felt a little silly, but this whole ordeal was about stretching myself. Rediscovering who I was. Not being afraid to be the odd one out. I actually thought I did a good job; it was just the lack of other costumes that made me uncomfortable. But Rue wouldn't have been uncomfortable, were she in my place. Rue didn't care what other people thought of her, or whether or not they liked her. I tried to emulate that. Fake it till you make it, right?

Half an hour after the faire started, my mind began to wander. What were the chances that Rue hadn't read any of my follow-up letters, and they'd all ended up in the trash?

Pretty good.

I had her number. She didn't *know* I had her number—I'd gotten it from Wyatt before deciding texting or calling her might not be the best move. No messages from her. I looked up her Facebook page. Friend request still pending. But that meant she hadn't outright rejected it, right?

Or she's just never on Facebook, I thought. She had every privacy setting Facebook offered turned on. I'd only found her account by sifting through Wyatt's friends.

Eleven o'clock rolled around. I leaned back against my car, watching a family with a lot of kids, and then a teen couple, walk into the faire. Something was being announced on loudspeaker, but I was too far out to understand the words. It was followed by some cheers—I wondered what it was.

I could just enjoy the day by myself, I thought, massaging my sternum with a knuckle, trying to keep the cold sense of rejection from knotting up. It might look weird, but I didn't know anyone around here, so it didn't really matter, right?

I sucked in a deep breath and let it all out at once, clipping the end with a chuckle. *Karma, Lan.* Not just for Rue either. There were a lot of women, especially in my early twenties, who I hadn't respected the way I should have. I'd always taken things a little too casually. And I'd finally been on the receiving end of that, so. The quicker I learned my lesson, the quicker the universe would right itself and give me a break.

The sun was getting hot, so I opened the door of my Tesla, turned on the AC, and sat in the driver's seat with my legs hanging out, feet on the asphalt of the parking lot. Okay, maybe I wouldn't stay. It seemed like fun, but I was suddenly . . . not in the mood. I'd wait until noon, maybe. Or one, or two. Perhaps scrape up the guts to call and just get the outright rejection straight from her mouth, for closure. Drive to Culver's and order the greasiest thing on their menu. Take myself to a movie, then go to the gym and burn off the hurt and frustration until I couldn't feel my body anymore. That would help, a little.

It just sucked because I really liked Rue. When she'd responded to my letter—even if it was a quick response—I'd hoped. Really hoped. I would never tell anyone this, but

I'd been stupidly happy all night, like a teenager who'd just had his crush say yes to prom. I hadn't felt . . . giddy . . . like that in a while. Even with TaLeah.

That's probably why I sat there for another hour and a half, taking the time to answer emails and place a few phone calls. I felt like a candle slowly drowning in its own melted wax. I still hoped, but the flame was getting dimmer and dimmer—

Someone kicked my shoe. "Hey."

I sat up so quickly I hit my head on the sun visor. At first I thought one of the faire workers was coming to ask if I was lost, or maybe to move my car so paying customers could park, but after a couple of blinks, I realized it was *Rue*. Her hair was blue now, and she had on some graphic liner that made her eyes look almost like an anime character's, but it was *Rue*.

A noise came out of my mouth as my brain tried to kick into gear. Something similar to what Homer Simpson might have mumbled upon the sight of donuts.

Rue rolled her eyes. "Are we going or not?"

"Uh, yes." Liquid wax evaporated and the candle burned so bright I could feel its heat on the inside of my ribs. I went to stand and hit my head *again*, this time on the car's frame. I tried to cover a wince and shot out of the vehicle. "Yes, I, uh, thanks for coming." I looked her over. "You look great."

Not a lie either. She had a true billowing Renaissance shirt, the collar wide and ruffled, and a leather corset cinched tightly around her waist and her— *Don't look at her chest, don't look at her chest.* She wore her LARPing skirt and a pair of light blue tights beneath it, complete with slouching leather boots.

Her mouth twisted in amusement as she looked me over. "I will honestly say the effort is appreciated."

My brain was still misfiring—*Rue was* here—but after a second I realized she meant my outfit. Stepping away from my car, I modeled it. "Not bad, eh?"

She snorted. "Not bad for you, no. Is this Londry's new attire?"

I smiled. "I don't know, do paladins wear tights?"

She shrugged. Met my eyes. I grinned, and to my delight, her lips mirrored it, though she looked away as though embarrassed by the expression.

Taking a deep breath, I steeled myself. "Thank you for coming."

She shrugged. "I expect a turkey leg."

I nodded, trying not to be too ecstatic. "Before we go in, I want to explain myself—"

She folded her arms. "Please don't."

"Just quickly, then," I pressed, because I didn't want to go into any of this *pretending*. Acting like the bad parts hadn't happened or that I hadn't royally screwed up, even if I hadn't realized it at the time. "I got distracted, when I got home from my mission. There were so many people who wanted my attention—and that is not an excuse. I blew it. I knew I should have called you—"

She frowned. "Landry—"

"But I didn't. And then I started dating someone, and I did think about it, but it also felt too late to try, like it'd be too weird. So I didn't. And I'm sorry. And I realize what an asshat I was—"

"Are Mormons allowed to say *asshat*?" she asked, that beautiful mouth twisting up again.

I shrugged. "I think we get a couple curses a week free."

She didn't meet my eyes, but nodded. "I guess I . . . could have been nicer . . . about it."

"Nah." Now she did look at me, eyes vividly green in the afternoon light. I caught myself staring and added, "I deserved it."

She shrugged.

Now or never. I offered my elbow to her. "M'lady? I hear they have churros."

She tried to mask a smile as she put her hand on the crook of my arm. "Not historically accurate, but I shall partake."

I did my best to hide the hop in my step as we approached the flower arch and got our wristbands. Blue, just like our tights.

RUE

For a first-time local Ren faire, Springville did a pretty good job.

There was a placard promising a magic show at two and a "fire dance" at eight, a quartet of high-school-aged singers in simple gowns, and a duck pond with plastic ducks for kids. Half of it was like a farmers' market—people selling everything from radishes to pet treats to throwing knives. Though, admittedly, it was hard to focus on much of anything with Landry there.

It was like the Twilight Zone. Nostalgic but not. Fever-dreamish, in a way. Walking through a park with Landry Harrison was something I could not wrap my mind around, and I had to keep reminding myself to relax. To focus on the music and not his biceps pressed against my palm. To remind myself it was okay to smile.

We turned around a corner stall selling necklaces. I tilted my head subtly toward the woman behind the counter. "Bonnets are eighteenth century."

Landry turned toward me, and I felt like I'd pushed my mom's makeup tweezers into the electric outlet again, the way his closeness zinged through me. He smelled *really good*. Was that bourbon? "Huh?"

I gestured again. "Historically inaccurate."

He laughed, and it warmed me to make him laugh, though a tiny voice in the back of my head chided me for it. "I wouldn't even know. Pretty sure cutoffs and shoelaces are also historically inaccurate."

I smiled, looking down at his slapdash trunk hose. "Fortunately, I don't think anyone will notice."

"Nah, they'll just notice you."

My cheeks warmed. I must have made a face, because Landry sobered. "Sorry, too much?"

I took a deep breath. "No. It's okay." *I'm just not used to being flirted with,* I didn't say. I tried to settle myself with the compliment as we walked. My brain's instinct was to outright deny that Landry found me attractive. Like I'd told Blaine, guys like Landry didn't go for women like me. But I was starting to realize that was a limiting belief I had unknowingly secured over years. But it was scary to face it now. Like taking down an ugly poster when you weren't sure what lay underneath it.

A man and a woman, roughly our age, approached us

laughing. They were both in costume—I'd noticed a lot of the attendees didn't dress up, but these two had. Stopping us, the man asked, "Do you have the Crown of Belize?"

"The what?" Landry asked.

"Uh, no," I added. "What for?"

The guy snapped his fingers, disappointed, as his—ring check—wife answered, "You have to find all five artifacts to get a coin."

"What kind of coin?" Landry asked.

"It's a collector's coin from the city," she explained and slowly turned around, scanning the way. It was getting crowded. "I don't know where else to look. We only have the crown left!"

"Can I help?" Landry offered, to my surprise.

"Yeah," the guy said, "but we've looked everywhere—"

Landry backed up and cupped his hands around his mouth. "DOES ANYONE KNOW WHERE TO FIND THE CROWN OF BELIZE?"

Several heads turned our way; I put my hand up to shield the side of my face from the onlookers. But, lo and behold, an older man ran up and said, "It's over by the axe throwing."

The couple lit up. "Really? Thank you!" Then, to Landry, "Thank you!" and they ran off in the direction they had come.

"Wow," I said as Landry offered his elbow once more. "The power of extroversion."

He laughed. "Says the one with blue hair." He touched a curl, shooting sparks through my scalp. "I like it, though."

I eyed him. "More than pink?"

"Hmm . . ." He considered for a moment. "I'm not sure on that one. What about me?"

"What about you?"

"If you could change my hair to any color, what would it be?"

I rolled my eyes, but played along. "Fire-engine red."

"Really?"

"Yes, because it would look awful." I tried not to smile, but it came through anyway. *Just relax, Rue.*

An old woman with a staff came up, a stack of cards in her hands, and handed one to us before moving on. Turning it over in my hand, I read, BE ONE OF THE FIRST 25 TO FIND THE ARTIFACTS AND WIN A COLLECTOR'S COIN!

"Oh, here we go." I turned the card over. "Want to play?"

"Sure, we might still have a chance." He took the card and studied it. Chuckled. "This is so nerdy."

I paused my step. "We don't have to."

"Oh, no, that's not what I mean," he covered, then visibly shook himself. "I want to, it'll be fun. But it is a little, you know."

"You know"—I plucked the card from his hand—"you don't have to defend yourself for liking something that's not mainstream. Nerd is in, dude. Marvel movies and all that jazz."

He ran a hand back through his hair, and that weird feeling of false nostalgia and disbelief washed through me again. Like I was finally living out the date we'd planned eight years before, and all that nervous excitement I'd had trickled back.

"Different *levels* of nerd," he said.

"Agreed."

"But yeah, you're right." He dropped his hand. "So, let's . . . wait, is that a trebuchet?" His voice pitched up in eagerness.

I followed his line of sight to a toddler-bed-sized trebuchet at the edge of the park. It shot apples into a giant target backed by hay bales. "Yes it is."

"Awesome, come on!" He grabbed my hand this time, instead of offering his elbow. More electricity zipped through me like we were a closed circuit hooked up to a battery charged past full. My heart raced as I jogged with him to the trebuchet and stood at the back of a line only two people long.

I laughed. "The way to Landry's heart: medieval war machines. I'm surprised you know what it's called."

"Me too." He laughed, and when our turn came around, he let me go first.

I hated to admit it.

I really, *actually* hated to admit it.

But I was having fun with Landry.

After the trebuchet, I started to relax and be myself— take my white-knuckled grip off my would-haves and should-haves one finger at a time. He bought me a turkey leg, Coke, and a street corn, and we ate by an artificial stream and talked about all manner of things, from LARPing to embarrassing work stories to favorite high school teachers. We went to the magic show, and since the seating was full, we stood off to the side and watched. The magician was actually good—even from my angle, I couldn't detect his sleight of hand. After that, I went to the bathroom, and when I returned, Landry announced he had bought me something. I worried it was one of the gaudy necklaces we had passed earlier, but when he presented it to me, it was a four-inch knife with a handle carved to look like a rose vine.

"Oh wow, this is beautiful." I picked it up and carefully tested the blade.

He beamed. "You can keep it under your pillow and use it to attack stalkers."

"Why, were you planning to visit anytime soon?" Regret bubbled up, chasing the words, but Landry simply laughed. I relaxed. Landry was teasable. I needed people who were teasable.

We'd circled the faire twice when a man dressed in friar robes approached us with wide arms. "And here, a fine gentleman and his finer lady," he said in a British accent. "Just whom we've been looking for. Tell me, do you know the tradition of the handfast?"

I blanched. "Uh . . ."

"No," Landry spoke when I didn't. "What is it?"

The friar gestured behind him at a trailer altered to look like tiny medieval church. "It is an act of betrothal! A man and woman handfast one year before their wedding."

Landry gaped. "For real?"

"It's not real," said a kind-looking, long-haired woman approaching from the church, a reassuring look on her face. "But we've just redesigned our website and would love it if you'd let us use your picture!" She gestured to a tripod set up closer to the trailer. "We'll send you copies free of charge."

"Oh, neat." Landry looked at me. "Want to try?"

I bit my lower lip. ". . . Sure," I managed, and the enthusiastic friar guided us closer to the "church."

"Welcome friends, family, all those dear to these," he said, speaking to a nonexistent crowd. One or two people slowed as they passed, curious, and I avoided the gaze. "We come together to celebrate the union of . . ." He gestured to Landry.

"Landry," he said.

"And . . ." He gestured to me.

I got that this wasn't real, but it was very wedding-like and kind of public and with a guy I barely . . . well, no. I actually knew Landry really well. But the warming-up period had only just ended and—

"Anastene," Landry filled in for me, offering me a small smile.

I blinked at him, and tight muscles in my back and shoulders slowly unwound. *Anastene*. Had he been able to see my discomfort? The friar prattled on, but I barely heard him. I just looked at Landry—then at the camera when directed—in awe.

He'd known. He somehow knew that I needed to play a part for this. That Anastene would be fine lying to a priest to meet her end goal. And mention of her name reminded me that *this was a just a game*. This was fun. It was meant to be fun.

The friar had us clasp hands—Landry's were warm and dry and large—and he wrapped a shimmery cord around them, all the way up to our elbows. I heard the click of the camera and wondered what the pictures would look like when we got the digital copies. If I'd adore them, laugh at them, or wish this moment had never happened.

I hoped it wouldn't be the last.

"Having spent time with Landry and Anastene," the friar went on, "I witness to the evidence of their connected souls."

I forced myself to keep a straight face. I didn't even know the guy's name, but it was all for the sake of the faire, so I went with it. Landry's eyes glimmered in good humor.

"It's in the way Anastene smiles." The friar smiled and

gestured to me. "Or the way she lights up at the mention of Landry's name."

My stomach clenched.

"It's in the gleam of Landry's eye when he speaks of the future, or the way he holds Anastene's hand on their way through the woods."

Or to the trebuchet.

"There is no denying the connection of these souls, and that is what we've come together to celebrate, here in this moment. The love that Landry and Anastene share between their spirits."

The camera clicked. The friar went through the declaration of intent and announced a nonexistent wedding date a year from now, then thanked us and had us sign a photo release. I finished mine first—Landry was reading all the fine print—and handed it over, taking the moment to lean against the fake church and study him, thinking about the scripted ceremony. And what, maybe, the friar should have said if he'd known our story.

Originally, I liked Landry because he'd been an outlet for me. Someone on the outside, someone uninvolved, who listened without judgment. He was kind and paid attention to me. Open and so sure of himself—something I really wanted to be.

But now? I studied the crease of his brow as he read the last paragraph of the photo release and clicked the pen to sign.

Now . . . I liked that he was still kind, still nonjudgmental, and yes, I suppose I liked the attention too. But I also liked that he recognized and accepted his mistakes. Yes, he definitely had an ego, but he had decent reins on it. He was adventurous and tenacious. I knew he was spiritual, but he never preached to me, which I appreciated. He was willing to try new things—as one could see from the women's navy knee-highs he had snug around his calves.

My stomach unclenched, and in doing so seemed to balloon up my heart, corny as that sounds. But Landry finished signing, gave the paper and a grin to the friar, and turned back to me, looking at me like I was the only girl at the faire, and I felt myself crack, like my chest was made of concrete struck by a hammer.

I was worried that if I fell, the cement blocks would cave in and crush me.

Chapter 12

WERE THIS A legit Ren faire, we could have stayed until dark. As it was, we ran out of things to do fairly quickly, even with the artifact hunt (yes, we won a coin, but we ended up giving it to a little girl in a princess costume).

We headed out to the parking lot around 4:00, and at some point along the way, my hand had moved from Landry's elbow to his hand, and it was weird but also . . . fine.

"How's Herospect?" he asked, scanning for my SUV before I pointed it out to him.

"Pretty good. Almost done."

"Too late to come back in?"

I shrugged. "It's never too late; Rhonda is really good at making things work. But next week is our last game for this campaign." I hesitated for a moment before saying, "But you could work on your character for the next campaign."

His pretty blue eyes lit up at the subtle invitation. "Yeah? Maybe I should stay a paladin. I don't really know anything about the rest."

"I could show you a website that has a lot of information," I offered. "I really like playing a rogue, but I think I'm going to do a fighter next time. I was a magic user last year and it's fun enough, but not very hands on."

"Huh. Maybe I should be a magic user." We reached my Nissan; I lingered by the driver-side headlight. Pulled my fingers from his and folded my arms.

"Scared of the foam swords?" I laughed.

"When Cameron is wielding them, I am," he said in mock defense. "He's intense."

I shrugged. "He's all right. Just doesn't like you."

He leaned against the hood. "He *definitely* likes you."

I sighed. "Too bad for him."

"Not a surprise for you?"

"I tend to attract the hard-headed type." I poked him in the chest, which should have been a casual gesture, but it felt weirdly intimate with Landry. "There's a couple different kinds of magic users. Actually"—I looked him up and down, sizing him up—"I might have a couple things that would fit you, if you want help with the costume."

"Yeah?" He sounded genuinely excited. I still couldn't wrap my head around a jock-type salesman being into role-play. "That would be awesome. I mean, you've seen my skills." He gestured to his costume. One of his trouser legs had come untied.

I chuckled. "You've just morphed into a ruined nobleman instead of a prosperous one." I checked my phone for the time. "If you want to swing by, I can grab them for you. The sooner you know your character story, the better."

"Today?"

I met his eyes. God help me, he was pretty. "Yeah, sure. You can follow me back in that fancy robot car."

He grinned, his smile bright enough to power a small country. "Can do."

I had a lot to think about on the way home.

I really liked Landry. I felt like a moth drawn to the flame—but the question of whether that flame was an innocent porch light or a bug zapper still scared me. How long would this last? What if I was just a temporary conquest, and he moved on to someone new next week?

I'd browsed his Facebook page. He had lot of female friends. Lots of options.

But how many guys try this hard for a one-time conquest? And what kind of conquest are we talking?

He wasn't just trying to get into my pants. I knew a lot about his beliefs from Wyatt, and he was definitely a wait-until-marriage kind of guy. He wasn't after my vagina. Just my heart.

That might have been worse.

He's chasing you, Blaine had said.

"I gave myself permission to do this," I said as I turned onto my street, glancing into the rearview mirror to see Landry behind me. "I have permission."

God help me, I was so scared.

I pulled into the driveway; Landry parked on the street by the mailbox, but it was late enough in the day for it not to be a problem. I slid out of my car and shuffled through my pockets for my keys.

"Your house looks like a gingerbread house," Landry said, coming up the sidewalk. "Just needs white trim."

I paused and looked over it. "Huh, it kind of does, doesn't it?" It was a rambler with brown stucco and white support poles jutting up from the small porch.

"Who owns the Accent?" He gestured to the black Hyundai parked on the side of the house.

"My neighbors." I pushed the key into the lock and turned it. "I'm in the upstairs, they're in the downstairs."

"They nice?" He followed me inside.

"They leave me alone, so they're perfect." I dropped my keys on the counter, then turned around. Something about Landry Harrison being *in my house* compacted my nerves. This was real. He was real. He was here. For me.

My mouth went dry, and all possibilities of something to say fled my mind.

Fortunately, Landry saved me. "Do you mind if I use your bathroom?"

"Y-Yeah. I mean, no, I don't mind. Well, maybe a little." I laughed, more of a nervous laugh than anything else. "Second door on the right." I gestured down the hallway.

"I'll put the seat down," he promised.

He left, and I escaped into my room, glancing at myself in the mirror. I smoothed flyaways in my hair. Considered changing, but this corset would take a hot second, and I didn't want to make Landry wait on me. Besides, I looked hot in it, so.

Instead, I went to my closet, desperate to busy myself, and pulled out some totes, sifting through them for costume pieces. I found a belt I'd gotten at a local thrift store that was insanely wide with an enormous silver buckle on it. Pulled it out, along with some shoe toppers that made regular shoes look like boots. A lot of my costuming stuff was feminine, but I had a cloak that might work for Landry, and behind a set of drawers was the staff I'd used when I was a wizard, a purple scarf still tied to it. By the time I gathered the things, Landry was back in the kitchen, hands in his pockets, looking around the room.

"You just move here?" he asked when I returned, then lifted an eyebrow at my collection. "Wow, that's a lot of stuff."

"You have no idea." I dropped the armful on the couch. "And no, I've been here for years. Why?"

He shrugged. "Not a lot of pictures."

"Yeah . . . I'm mostly incredibly lazy."

He chuckled. "I get that. So"—he clapped his hands—"what do you got for me?"

An egg sac full of moths tore open in my gut. *You gave yourself permission.*

And then the answer popped into my head like it'd been spring-loaded. My thoughts swirled back to Blaine's bridal shower. Back to Courtney and her Lexus.

I must have taken a few extra seconds to process it all, because Landry dipped to the side so his face was in front of mine. "Rue?"

I blinked. Right. Time to settle this.

Pointing to the couch, I said, "Sit."

Landry's gaze shifted between the couch and me, but he didn't question me, just sat. Point one for him. Pulling out my phone, I googled *Neuroscience questions love staring*, because I didn't know exactly what it was called.

Fortunately, Google did. It pulled up a *New York Times* article, which linked to a paper titled "The Experimental Generation of Interpersonal Closeness: A Procedure and Some Preliminary Findings."

"Rue?"

"Hold," I said, scrolling through, finding the questions in the appendix. There were a few sets of them, more than the thirty-six the *NYT* article promised, but I went for it. Phone still in front of my face, I moved to the couch. Landry sat on its far end, and all my costuming stuff took up the rest of the space.

So I sat on Landry.

His back straightened. "Hello," he said, more shocked than anything else, because I sat forward-facing on his lap, straddling him, but I didn't sit up close enough for any groin contact, for his sake. I knew the Latter-day Saint rules, thanks to my brother. Landry tensed for a couple second before relaxing. I was still glued to my phone, so he asked, "What's up?"

"Questions," I said. "It's very scientific." I turned my phone around so he could see the bland black-and-white of the paper. Turned it back to myself. I read through several of them, wishing I had the exact thirty-six the *NYT* deemed the most important. I used my best judgment and tried not to think about Landry's thighs pressing into mine. I only kind of succeeded.

"Before making a telephone call"—my voice had a slight rasp in it, and I cleared my throat—"do you ever rehearse what you're going to say, and why?"

He blinked at me. "Is this an interview?"

I considered. "Yes."

He nodded, like it was totally acceptable that I'd trapped him in my house, sat on him, and started berating him with questions without any lead-up. Another point for him. And his thighs. "Sometimes," he answered.

I frowned.

"It depends," he amended, and pushed off the couch to adjust. I was impressed he could lift me so easily. Another point. "If it's a sales call or something like that, then yeah, I rehearse. Sometimes I write down the bullet points of what I need to say. With people, usually not. Unless I'm nervous about the call for some reason." He studied my face. "Like if I were trying to ask a woman to dinner who had already turned me down before, I would probably definitely rehearse what I was going to say beforehand."

I couldn't help but smirk at that.

"If you were able to live to the age of ninety," I moved on, feeling warm from our close proximity, "and retain either the mind or body of a thirty-year-old for the last sixty years of your life, which would you want?"

"Mind," he said without hesitation.

His answer surprised me. "Really?" I poked his biceps. Also firm, unsurprisingly.

He relaxed back into the couch. "I want to be healthy physically, of course, but what's the point of living a good life if you can't remember it?"

Touché.

"I watched my grandpa fade away," he went on, quieter. "Alzheimer's. It sucked. It really sucked for my mom. He couldn't remember who she was at the end. Sometimes he'd call her by my grandma's name. On occasion he'd walk out of the house and get lost, and we'd have to call the police and drive around the neighborhoods looking for him. He was like that for about ten years." He rubbed a hand down his face. "It wasn't a good life."

The story made my heart heavy. "I'm sorry."

"Thanks. What about you?"

"Mind," I answered truthfully. "Same reasons, though I don't have an Alzheimer's story."

He set his hand on my leg, and shivers swept up it like it was falling asleep. I tried to focus on the matter at hand . . . but I didn't push it away.

Turning back to my phone, I scrolled around. "Tell your partner what you like about them."

A sly, canine grin stretched on his face. "Are you my partner, then?"

I gave him what I hoped was a withering look. "For the sake of this exercise, yes."

He rubbed his thumb up and down my calf, which was *incredibly* distracting. Every upward stroke was a burst of chills, every downward a flash of heat. "I like that you don't care what others think of you. I like that you live unapologetically to the beat of your own drum. I like that you're kind, but you mask it with sarcasm because you don't want anyone to know."

I straightened. "What?"

"Do you deny it?"

I chewed on the inside of my lip. "No . . . but you don't *like* that."

"I do, though." Now he squeezed my leg. His hand was warm. "I can tell you're fiercely loyal, to your friends, family, and to yourself. I like that you're adventurous. I like that you're forgiving."

My cheeks warmed at that last one.

"And I like this." He gestured with his non-leg-squeezing hand to my general person.

I cleared my throat. "The corset or my figure?"

He searched my face, perhaps gauging how honest he should be. "Both."

"Hmm." Turning off my phone screen, I set it aside. My cheeks warmed even more, but fair was fair. "I like . . . that you listen."

He smiled.

"You listen and you don't judge me," I added, averting my eyes. "I like that you put effort into every part of your life—at least, the parts I've seen so far. Including me. I *don't* like"—I met his eyes again—"that you spell the word *weird* wrong. The rest I can ignore, but that one just . . ." I clucked my tongue.

He laughed. "How do you spell it?"

"W-E-I-R-D."

"I before E, except after C," he began.

"That rule actually applies to the minority of I-E words," I countered.

He looked at me like I had a halo or something. "Does it now?"

My pulse was visible in my neck. It had to be. I could certain hear its echo in my ears.

I grabbed my phone.

"More questions?" he asked.

"Skipping the questions," I said, pulling up my clock app. "The end of this is supposed to be staring at each other for four minutes." *Ugh.* This was going to be . . . painful. But it was supposed to be meaningful too, so . . . I could deal.

"Seriously?"

"Yep. In the eyeballs." I feigned assertiveness, set the countdown, and hit start. Braced myself on the couch's armrest and stared at his eyes.

He didn't question me. Didn't make fun of me. Just participated.

Four minutes *was* a really long time. We stared and stared, and I was tempted to check my phone, to see how much time was left, but that would break the spell. And it was a spell—like the wizarding items sitting next to us had a little bit of real spark in them, and it was permeating the room. I stared at Landry's eyes, deciding they were cerulean, specifically, with a little bit of brown edging around the iris. His eyelashes were darker than his hair. His pupils were dilated. The heat in my cheeks trickled down my neck, shoulders, and chest, and after a couple minutes, I felt like I was falling down into those eyes, like a bottomless pit, but . . . I wasn't afraid. It was a darkness like drawn curtains when I was finally lying down to sleep after a long day or the black of a theater wall right before the movie started. It was a comfortable darkness. A cozy one.

And sitting there on his lap, on my couch, so close to him, I . . . fit. Like our legs and this furniture were custom made specifically for this moment. And more moments, if I chose. I felt that very distinctly, like it flowed through my veins. This was my choice. I knew, by the way he looked at me, that Landry had already chosen.

My organs felt too big for my body. My skin too warm. My hair follicles prickled.

The timer went off. I blinked.

Then I leaned forward and kissed him.

This time, Landry didn't startle. He reacted like he'd expected it. His lips were full and warm, and like the couch and our legs, they fit perfectly against mine. We were two negative—or maybe positive—ends meeting, sparking, flashing.

His hand abandoned my leg and cupped the side of my face—another perfect fit. I tried to ignore my heart booming like a timpani—or was that his heart?—and tilted my head to the side for better leverage, which encouraged him. He pushed off the back of the couch and really *kissed* me, warm and wet and sweet. It sent fiery jolts through my skull and down my arms, and I wondered if I'd really ever kissed anyone, because none of my previous experience compared to this. It was magic. Real-life magic, not pretend. Not role-play.

After . . . at least *another* four minutes . . . Landry pulled back suddenly, grabbed my phone, and turned the alarm off.

Then he grasped me by the waist and kissed me again as I laughed into his mouth, full and fixed and delightfully happy.

Chapter 13

LANDRY

I FELT LIKE I was in a Hallmark movie.

Everything was just so . . . perfect. I mean, Hallmark movies usually didn't feature big brown mountains with everything dying in the August heat and gathering pollution because the valley was in dire need of rain, but as far as Rue went . . . I couldn't ask for anything more, especially when I'd expected so much *less*.

But Rue—it was like a switch flipped. She'd forgiven me and she liked me and she said yes when I asked her to dinner Tuesday night. We started texting (she was really into inappropriate GIFs). She invited me to her roller derby game on Wednesday, and heaven help me, she looked amazing in fishnets. I would see an image of Rue in a helmet and fishnets behind my eyelids for the rest of my life.

(Best player on the team, if I do say so myself. We decided my derby name was PhiLANDRYpist. Get it? Not that I'm going to skate anytime soon . . .)

Herospect had scheduled their final campaign day for Friday, since their campaign-end party was Saturday, and apparently last weekend's game was cut short. So right after work I drove to Rue's house, and we carpooled in her Nissan to the park. I talked to Rhonda on the phone Thursday evening, and we decided to have Londry be a henchman for the main villain, so she superpowered my character and planned to have the team fight me before the final battle. I was no expert in foam swordplay, but she gave me a *ton* of hit points, so I wasn't too worried about it.

Funny. Even just a few months ago, I might have cringed at the idea of playing make-believe in the park. Now I was weirdly excited for it. Rue and I talked LARP and our next characters on the drive there, and it was incredibly hard not to spill the beans that Londry was going to betray everyone as soon as Rhonda gave the signal.

We pulled into a parking spot. I always wanted to open Rue's door for her, but she'd blankly told me it was stupid to wait on someone to do something she could do herself, so I held off. I grabbed the cloak she was loaning me from the back seat. Wore my oversize dress shirt from the Renaissance faire.

"Don't be sad if you die," Rue said, flicking a strand of wavy blue hair out of her eye as we walked to the grass.

"Oh, I won't be." I couldn't help the grin splitting my face.

She paused. "What do you know, Landry Harrison?"

A new voice asked, "Oh, he's back?" and didn't try very hard to hide the contempt.

I glanced over to see Cameron at the edge of the field, his foam hammer hanging off his belt by a leather cord, his arms folded across his thick chest, frowning at me. I waved a hand. "Hey, Cameron. How are ya?"

And then casually laced my fingers through Rue's.

He definitely noticed. Eyes dipped down; expression darkened. "Good enough. Guess you're NPCing again?"

"PC," Rue answered. Rhonda blew her whistle, so Rue released my hand and smacked my backside. I had a different starting time than the others, since I had to rejoin the party. Focusing on Cameron, she jerked her head toward the other players. "Come on, we've got a Gorgon to kill."

Cameron passed one more glare my direction before following after Rue like a kicked puppy. I sighed. *It's fine,* I told myself and sought out Rhonda, who directed me toward the same copse of trees where I'd started out at as a temple keeper. Only this time, they were "just forest," as she put it.

It took the group thirty minutes to get to me, so I spent the time answering some work emails on my phone. When they approached, I quickly went through their names in my head—that salesman trick would *always* prove useful.

"Is that Londry I see?" asked Adelaide, playing Justine, in a British accent.

"I think so," replied her real-life husband Thom, and not-in-game husband Derek. Wait, no, Dyrek. I remembered that one because his pants were bright blue, so *dyed.* Dyrek.

Cameron/Drakon grumbled, "So he decides to show his face again?"

"The warders needed him," Rue/Anastene said, relaying backstory Rhonda had put together to make my absence work for the game.

I approached, holding up my hand in greeting. "You've made it! I worried you'd gotten hurt." I didn't try an accent or anything. I needed a lot more practice—and maybe a re-watch of the Harry Potter movies—before I'd feel confident doing that.

"No thanks to you," spat Cameron/Drakon.

I wasn't surprised he was giving me grief, so I just ignored him. Scanned the group until I saw the scroll in Johnny/Rell's hands. "Is that what I think it is?"

The wizard glanced at the scroll. "You know this?"

"The Scroll of Anarsa." I'd taken copious notes from my call with Rhonda and memorized everything. I didn't want to hold up the game because I fudged something. And, honestly, I wanted to impress Rue.

Glancing her way, I saw she seemed pleased. Excellent.

"Yes," I went on. "It's been . . . years since I've seen that symbol."

McKenzie/Chaylock, the team healer, said, "Do you know where it's from?"

Rue/Anastene added, "We're trying to find the author. It's critical to our mission."

"Is it?" Rhonda told me to play coy. That was pretty coy, right?

"Don't tell him anything." Cameron/Drakon took a step forward and hefted his hammer, trying to be intimidating. "I don't trust him."

In this case, Drakon was correct in doing so.

But McKenzie/Chaylock put a hand on his hammer and lowered it. "He's a servant of the gods, Drakon. If we re-fused to trust everyone you found suspicious, we'd still be in Fleethollow."

No idea what Fleethollow was. But man, these guys were amazing actors. If I ignored the cars driving past and the kids on the playset, I felt like I was filming a movie.

"I know, if you need a guide," I said and pointed in a random direction. We walked in circles for long travels, since we had to stay in the park. "It's a tremulous path."

I glanced at Rue, hoping she'd be impressed with my vocabulary. She met my eyes for a minute, hiding a smile, before looking into the distance.

"We don't have many options," she said.

"We should search him first," Cameron/Drakon added.

Adelaide/Justine stepped forward. "Should we search you too?"

Cameron seemed put off by that.

The group agreed to follow me, so I led them past the copse of trees. Rhonda joined us, walking about twenty feet ahead, and I essentially followed her, weaving back toward the playset—where the high schoolers leapt out at us, pretending to be ogres. We fought them off and continued on our way, returning, eventually, to the copse of trees, which Rhonda announced was a copper-gilded door pressed between trunks, and from where we stood, there seemed to be nothing beyond it. Atop it was a message written in the ancient tongue.

"Oh." Rue dug through her satchel for her decoder. "I can translate—"

"No need." I tried to sound evil. Probably didn't do a great job, but hey, I was a beginner. "Your journey ends here."

The group froze. "What?" asked Rue/Anastene at the same time Thom/Dyrek asked, "What are you doing?"

I drew my foam sword, on loan from Rhonda. "I will

sever your bones from your body for the dark one to feast upon."

Behind us, Rhonda added flavor: "His eyes flash black, and you see dark scales forming over his hands and neck."

Rue swore. "He's a fiend."

"I knew it!" Cameron/Drakon pulled his hammer and came at me.

My sword had a longer range, so it wasn't hard to lightly hit him in the side. He ignored it and struck me in the shoulder.

Rhonda called out, "You're down, Drakon."

"What?" He whirled around, sounding genuinely pissed off. "He's a level-two paladin!"

But Rhonda merely shook her head. "Nope. He's a level-fourteen fiend, and that blade is poisoned."

Many more curse words spread throughout the group. With a sour face, Cameron/Drakon lay on the grass. The group, well practiced with combat, spread out.

"I'll draw him away!" Adelaide/Justine announced. "Chaylock, get to Drakon!"

My eyes flicked to Rue, who stuck her tongue out at me before drawing her daggers.

Adelaide and Thom both charged at me. Rhonda had to call out damage for me, since I was being ganged up on. Rue's little daggers flew through the air, one getting me in the head, one missing. A minute later Cameron/Drakon was back on his feet, and McKenzie/Chaylock was working on getting Thom/Dyrek alive again. Johnny/Chell cast spells from the back. I was too focused on swinging to see him, but Rhonda called out things like, "Your freeze spell doesn't work" or "Londry, you take ten fire damage!"

The whole ordeal lasted less than five minutes, and I

dramatically died between the trees. Adelaide/Justine helped herself to my sword, and Rue went through my pockets, taking the plastic gemstones Rhonda had given me that morning.

As I got up to join the NPCs, I heard McKenzie/Chaylock say, "I don't have any spell points left" to Cameron, who was again lying on the grass. Were this a real fight, he would be dead and in pieces. Guy was all offense.

"No potions?" he asked, despite the fact that he was supposed to be unconscious.

She shook her head before looking to the others. "Health potions?"

They pulled out inventory lists, and one by one shook their heads.

"Damnit, Cameron," Rue said, hands on her hips. "You should have been more careful! Now we're down a man for the final battle."

Cameron looked pleadingly at Rhonda. "It's the final battle!"

Rhonda shrugged. "You know the game rules. You can join the NPCs."

Setting his jaw, Cameron shot me a dark look, which I ignored.

The rest of the party performed a death ritual for their fallen comrade—McKenzie cried *real tears*—before Rue solved the puzzle and got the door open. The rest of the time I played various evil minions, then sat back as they fought the final boss, the dark one, which was played by the three teens with their arms linked to portray one enormous beast. All three wore purple sashes, so a lot of magic was thrown around.

But the time eight o'clock rolled around, the dark one had

been vanquished, the campaign was over, and we all sat in a circle speaking of what our characters accomplished over the next several years—basically personal epilogues to complete each player's story. Well, everyone but Cameron, who was dead and brooded about it the entire time.

The guy had to be at least my age. But hey, I didn't make the rules. He should take it up with Rhonda. He ducked out early, either to lick his wounds or to use the bathroom—I hadn't been paying attention.

"Potluck tomorrow at noon!" Rhonda reminded everyone, which reminded *me* I needed to get ingredients for soup. I was a decent chef, but there were a few dishes I felt like I did well. Lobster bisque was one of them (and honestly, as soon as you say *lobster*, people assume it's fancy, despite the fact that they're eating tasteless sea bugs).

"You turd." Rue lightly punched my shoulder while everyone packed up.

I laughed. "Not mad at me?"

"What? No, that was awesome." She brushed grass off her skirt and stretched. "Best acting you've ever done."

"Yeah?"

She nodded. "It wasn't *good*, but good enough."

"Uh-huh." I pushed her shoulder, then grabbed her hand and pulled her back as we headed toward the parking lot. "Not sure I can summon *actual tears* like McKenzie." I said it loud enough for her to hear, and she turned around, grinning, offering a wave. "I might have to pack lemon slices for that."

Rue winced. "Maybe make your character a stoic."

We reached her car; I opened the back seat and shoved my cloak and her sword in there, then heard her curse from the driver's side.

"What's wrong?" I jogged around.

Rue knelt by the front tire, which was flatter than the Florida shoreline. "This is fantastic."

I whistled and crouched next to her, checking the treads. "These look new."

"They are."

"Warranty?"

"I don't remember." She ran her hand over the tire, uncaring about the dirt. "I think the receipt is in my glove box."

"You have AAA or anything?"

"Do I look like someone who has AAA?" She puffed a blue lock out of her face. "Oh, jeez."

She found a nail in the side of the tire. Grabbed it and yanked until it slid out.

"Yikes," I offered. "Let's put the spare on and get my car."

Shame softening her features, she said, "I, uh . . . don't have a spare."

I blinked. "All cars usually come with one."

"Yeah . . . I already used it . . . a while ago. It's not in the trunk. I know that much."

I let out a long breath. "Well, we can tow it—"

Cameron's voice slipped over our heads. "I can give you a ride, Rue."

Turning around, I shielded setting sun from my eyes and looked up at Cameron. Seemed his wounds were thoroughly licked.

"Hey, thanks." Rue stood and stretched her back. "I appreciate it. I'm in Lehi."

"I know."

To me, she said, "Come on."

But Cameron put out a hand as I stood, like he was a

traffic cop and I was a teenage driver inching into the intersection. "Sorry, I only have space for one. But you can wait, right?"

I wasn't sure if there was a hint of smugness in the question or if I was imagining it.

Rue scoffed. "Cam, you drive a Honda Pilot. How do you not have space?"

Recoiling slightly, he said, "I have a lot of gear in the back."

Rue rolled her eyes and pulled out her phone. "It's fine. Tow is expensive. I'll just get us an Uber and see if that spare is in the garage." She glanced at me. "Do you have anything else today?"

"Just you," I said with a smile, pointedly not looking at Cameron. I had a feeling Rue wouldn't take well to me alpha-maleing on him.

"Hey, uh, no, it's fine." Cameron shielded Rue's Uber app with his hand, drawing her attention back to him. "I'll move some stuff around. Come on."

"Thanks." She passed me a curious look, a sort of shrug with her eyebrows. She followed him down a few spaces to a black Honda Pilot. Cameron made a show of opening the back door and shuffling stuff around, but I was taller than he was—I could see over his shoulder. He didn't have that much stuff. Duffel bag, dog blanket, several empty Monster cans. Cooler in the trunk.

I rolled my neck. *Not worth stressing over.* I really hated drama, so I said nothing.

Rue also hated drama, which I appreciated to an extreme level. TaLeah had lived for it.

Rue offered me the passenger seat, but Cameron butted

in with, "Ladies first." Not that I would have put her in the back seat, anyway. We slid in, buckled, and Rue typed her address into Cameron's GPS.

"So what character are you playing next?" he asked.

Rue told him about Lukartha, the "dragon-ilk" character she was putting together.

"You know what," I said, "I just realized something. You like characters with complex makeup."

Rue glanced back at me, considering. "Huh, I guess I do. I need to test out some shading stuff for the scales—"

"I might try being a healer," Cameron said over her, never glancing my way. "I know it's kind of a girl thing, but it might be fun."

A line formed between Rue's brows. "Why is it a girl thing?"

"You know. In video games and stuff. It's always a girl." He glanced over. "That is, uh, McKenzie is a girl."

"She's twenty-six."

"So?"

"So she's a woman," Rue said, not rudely, just matter-of-factly.

Leaning forward, I asked, "Does Rhonda regulate the characters? Like, to make sure you're not all wizards?"

"We usually discuss it enough that that doesn't happen," she explained. "Because it wouldn't be fun for *us* if we were all the same thing. Though"—she grinned—"we have talked about all being bards and making it a musical."

I laughed. "Oh man, I would *have* to see that."

"Which exit do I turn on?" Cameron spoke a little too loudly, and asked despite the path being clearly laid out on the GPS.

Internally shrugging, I leaned back against my seat and mostly listened to the rest of the conversation. Cameron obviously didn't want to talk to me so he could spend the next fifteen minutes chatting with Rue. But he'd have to work a *lot* harder than that to turn her eye.

I knew from experience.

Chapter 14

RUE

CAMERON WAS BEING weird.

Edit: weirder than usual.

"I really don't mind." He leaned across the front seats of his Pilot in a way that looked uncomfortable, inching closer and closer to the passenger seat window he'd rolled down. "It's not that out of the way."

"Did you move?" I couldn't help the deadpan tone in my voice. Landry was definitely out of the way. Salt Lake City was out of the way for anyone who didn't live in Salt Lake City.

Cameron ignored the question and, for the first time since dying on the field, addressed Landry directly. "I'll give you a ride. Just trying to be a Good Samaritan."

And, once again, Landry said, "My car is right there," and pointed to the Tesla parked by my mailbox.

Finally understanding it was a (weird and) losing battle, Cameron said goodbye and pulled out of my driveway too slowly. Landry and I were in the house by the time he finally rolled over the curb.

"Wonder what sour apple he ate," I muttered, tossing my keys on the counter.

"He likes you," Landry said.

Spinning around, I leaned back against the counter and flicked my hair. "Doesn't everyone?"

He smiled like he was in a men's fashion magazine and closed the distance between us, putting his hands on my waist and kissing me lightly. "You should try being pricklier. Might help," he said against my mouth. Pulling back, he added, "Garage?"

I sighed. "I haven't eaten yet." My stomach growled, and I glanced into the kitchen. "Let's make cheesecake."

He laughed, but the sound faded when I didn't. "You're serious? For dinner?"

"Didn't you LARP off a bunch of calories?"

"Calories are one thing," he countered, "timing is another. Good cheesecakes take hours, don't they?"

I usually made this weird microwave version from a 1980s cookbook I stole from my mom, and I had it down to twenty-three minutes. "Who said it was going to be good?" Rounding the counter, I hunted through my crammed cookbook cupboard to find the one I had in mind.

"You don't think . . ." Landry began, then stopped. Glancing back at him, I saw him run his hand back through his hair. It was getting long on top, and there was the slightest curl at the end of it.

"You should grow your hair out." I fought against the sudden urge I had to play with it.

He dropped his hand. "You don't think *Cameron* put the nail in, did you?"

"What? No." Turning back to the cupboard, I found the chartreuse hardcover book and pulled it out. "He's a good guy, just quirky."

"Rue." He approached me slowly. "The nail was in the *side* of the tire. Kind of hard to run over something like that."

I paused, an uneasy feeling bubbling in my gut. "Yeah . . . and it was straight too." And clean . . . wasn't it? Where did I stick that thing? Setting the book down, I checked my pockets, but I must have left it at the scene of the crime.

"Maybe it was kicked up by another car," I said, more for myself than for him. "I've known Cameron for years . . . he's not psycho enough to do something like that."

"Yeah, you're probably right." He pulled up a stool and sat. "And what are the chances he just had a hammer and nail at the ready? Unless that duffel bag was a makeshift toolbox."

"What duffel bag?"

"In his back seat."

I rolled my eyes. "The back seat too full for a second passenger?" Shaking my head, I flipped through the cookbook's dessert section until I found my recipe. It required chilling, but I ran my freezer pretty cold. "Boy is subtle. Maybe I should set him up with someone."

"Maybe." Landry didn't sound convinced. "Probably shouldn't leave it unattended too long." He checked his watch. "I think Discount closes at nine, in case we can't find a spare. Grab McDonald's or something on the way?" He checked his pocket, then his other. Stood up and checked again. "Huh."

"What?"

"I don't have my phone. Did you grab it?"

I shook my head. "I didn't." Retrieving mine—remembering I was still in LARP garb when I saw the scales on the back of my hand—I should probably wash up before I went anywhere else—I called Landry's number. Listened.

"Is it on silent?" I asked. I doubted it—Landry always kept his ringer on because he was afraid of missing a work call.

"No. Text Cameron?"

I pulled up Cameron's contact and texted him.

> Hey, is Landry's phone in your backseat?

"He's driving," I said. "Might take a second to respond." I offered a sympathetic smile. "Maybe it's at the park."

"Yeah, maybe." He sighed. "Probably should get going sooner than later."

I pulled away from the cookbook, considering the offer. "Okay." I studied his suntanned face, all scrunched and rugged with worry. A grin wormed its way across my lips. "But can we make out first?"

Some of those worry lines popped away like a taut string cut. "Absolutely."

The nail wasn't bent, except a little on the head. Pretty clean too. Crouching next to my Nissan, I tossed it in the air and caught it a few times, wondering.

Landry tightened the last bolt on my spare, which we'd found under a box of Blaine's old stuff that she'd meant to donate before moving to Washington. "There ya go." He wiped sweat off his forehead and stood. Honestly, I expected him to dance around the tire a little bit or put down a towel or something. Landry didn't seem like someone who liked to get dirty. But looking at the grease smears on his hands and dirt on the knees of his jeans, I realized, yet again, that I'd judged him unfairly.

Made me wonder who else I'd mislabeled.

"You're a saint." I rose to my feet and kissed his cheek. Pocketed the nail and pulled out my phone. The parking lot was lit until eleven, but the field wasn't, so it was flashlight time. "Ready for Marco Polo?"

"As ever."

I pulled up his contact and clicked call. With luck, his phone would be faceup, and we'd see it when the screen lit up. "What's your ringtone for me, by the way?"

He flushed a little. "Uh . . . it's the default."

I leaned my weight onto one leg. "You have ringtones for everyone. Like it's 2005."

"Well, if we find it, you'll hear it." He winked and jogged toward the grass. I walked the length of the parking lot, listening, until the call went to voicemail. Then I hung up and tried again.

The weird thing about this situation—outside of the nail— was that Landry's GPS wasn't working either. He'd looked it up on my laptop. His phone had been turned off, so it only had its last known location—which was this park. Unless he switched it off and then lost it elsewhere, but Landry claimed he never turned his phone off. Thus our attempting to call it regardless.

I turned mine off all the time, but potato-tomato—whatever the saying was.

I called, hung up, called, hung up. Left a sultry voice message that might get me in trouble when he finally listened to it. Walked the length of the entire park, looking with my eyes more than my ears. I posted in the Herospect Facebook group, asking if anyone had seen it, but no one had. Rhonda even looked through her extra gear. It had just . . . vanished.

My phone buzzed—Cameron texting me back. *No, I haven't. Have you asked on the FB page?*

Another dead end.

After about an hour of searching, Landry walked up to me, defeated. "I don't know, babe. I might have to bite the bullet and get another one." He sighed. "This is really annoying."

I touched his arm. "At least you can do email and texts on your laptop."

"Yeah." He rubbed his jaw, where stubble was regrowing. I wondered if I could convince him to grow out a beard. Landry was too clean cut for my liking . . . though maybe not, since I liked him anyway. A little more, every day. It was exhilarating and terrifying.

Was this how Mormons ended up getting married so quickly?

"You called me babe," I said flatly.

He started. "Did I? Sorry."

I pinched him. "I don't *hate* it." I pushed my own phone into my pocket and glanced around, wondering if I'd get a glint of a screen somewhere in the expansive lawn, but alas, the phone didn't present itself. "I'll treat you to some pancakes." We still hadn't made it to McDonald's. "Pick a diner."

He leaned on me dramatically. "Thank you."

I tried to walk away, but he was *heavy*. "You're welcome, you nerd."

"How about"—he straightened slowly—"instead of *babe*, I call you *maneater*."

I wrinkled my nose. "Maneater? Why?"

His eyes took on a mischievous glint. "Because that's your ringtone."

"You butthole!" I shouted, and he took off toward my newly repaired SUV. I chased after him. "I hope you never find that phone!"

The Event of the Year was today.

No, not the Met Gala.

Rhonda usually hosted the annual LARP party at her house, since she had a large family room and a patio, but smoke from California forest fires was smogging up the air pretty badly, so we opted for inside.

A newcomer might have thought that Rhonda decorated for the occasion—an entire wall was full of display weapons (some real), and a set of three samurai swords sat atop the mantel. The opposite wall was mortared cobblestone with a cloth family crest and Viking helmet hanging from it. A large carpet mimicked the art style of 1200s England. But no, this was just how Rhonda's house looked. She was hard core.

If I ever had the money to do something like this to a house I owned, I absolutely would.

I came in with my tray of mandatory bacon-tomato cups and a giant tray of cupcakes, because regardless of what Rhonda said, potlucks were better with excessive amounts of dessert. My mom had taken some cake-decorating classes with me as a teen, which was a long time ago, so my cupcakes looked nice, but hardly professional. Not that it mattered—I'd stuffed every one of these suckers with three Rolos before baking. They tasted amazing.

(I knew. I'd already had two.)

I'd come by myself—Landry said he'd meet me here because today was try-to-get-a-new-phone day, and regardless of carrier, that always took hours. But it was almost noon, so I imagined he was just about finished up by now.

I set my tray and baking sheet on the table full of chips, dips, and pigs in a blanket as Cameron set down a giant bowl of ice for drinks. "Oh man"—he ogled the bacon-tomato cups—"those look amazing." His gaze switched to the cupcakes. "*Those* look amazing."

I grinned. "They *are* indeed amazing." Bacon with mayonnaise, also known as the god of all condiments? Check. Chocolate cupcakes topped with raspberry vanilla frosting? Check. What was not to love?

Cameron reached for a cupcake.

"Don't let Rhonda see." Rhonda was a stickler for party rules, just like my mom.

Fear flashed over his face, and Cameron pulled back. "Right. I don't need to die twice in one week."

I laughed. "Sorry about that."

He shrugged. "I was a little too excited, I guess. I decided on a tank for the next campaign, so hopefully I'll be harder to kill." He glanced around, and his face lit up. "Landry not coming?"

I side-eyed him. Boy needed some acting lessons. And a hint. "Coming late." I, too, surveyed the room. Everyone but Johnny had arrived. "He's getting a new phone."

"Bummer." He stuck his hands in his pockets. "Did he find it broken or never find it?"

"Never found it." I sighed. "People are turds. Some teen probably scooped it up and sold it on Craigslist. Fortunately, he had insurance on it."

"Sorry." He gestured to a coffee table where a few games were set up; Adelaide and Thom were lounging nearby on their phones. "Want to play Jenga?"

Johnny wasn't here yet, so why not? "Sure."

We knelt on the floor by the table and set up the tower; McKenzie swung by to start playing just as Johnny appeared with drinks. Rhonda was fiddling with a projector—she loved showing slideshows of our campaign before announcing what the new story line would be. I took a few turns pulling out blocks before glancing to the door. Landry had texted me from his computer last night, saying he was going in first thing in the morning because he didn't want to miss the party. On McKenzie's turn, I pulled out my phone and texted him.

New phone yet?

No response. My turn came. I pulled out the last middle block.

"You always take the easy way out," McKenzie complained.

"It's just playing smart." I elbowed her.

Cameron, for whatever reason, pulled out a load-bearing piece on the bottom, causing the tower to fall. "Whoops," he said, then pressed a hand to his abdomen. "Uh, sorry. Duty calls."

"Gross," McKenzie and I said in unison, but we set up the tower as he excused himself to the bathroom. We'd just finished when Rhonda stepped in front of us and clapped her hands.

"You have permission to dine," she announced. "Thank you for bringing the full food pyramid and not just desserts."

"Sweet." I stood and lent a hand to McKenzie; we were the first ones at the table. My phone buzzed while I was loading a bun with pulled pork. I hurriedly filled my plate before grabbing a seat on the couch and checking my texts. Landry was probably lost.

Yeah, new phone, he replied.

I texted, *How far out are you?*

The three dots at the bottom of my screen jumped as he texted back. I took a bite of pulled pork and rolled my eyes. Swallowing, I shouted to Rhonda, "This is *fantastic!*"

"Thank you," she smirked. "I watched my husband smoke it myself."

The three dots were still bouncing on my phone. Weird; Landry was a concise texter. I took another bite.

The text came through.

> Listen, I've been thinking. Please don't take offense to this.

I stopped chewing, my stomach sinking, like it knew what was happening before my brain did.

> LARP and all this nerd stuff isn't really for me. It's a big part of who you are. It IS who you are. I just

think . . . it's been fun, but maybe it's better that we
go our separate ways.

I swallowed hard, the half-chewed bite nearly cutting off
my airflow.

Landry was breaking up with me.

Chapter 15

I STARED AT my phone. And stared. And stared. As if scrutinizing the words long enough and letting my vision go in and out of focus would rearrange the letters. Or make a smiley emoji pop up with a big *JK* next to it.

After all this . . . after all the effort he put in, all the effort *I* put in . . . he was ending it? Like that? Over *text*?

Was the new phone just a ruse because he didn't have the backbone to face me in person?

My ribs felt like they were shrinking, like they were made of ice and dripping down my insides. My throat closed up. I blinked, pissed to hell that there were tears on my eyelashes. I reread the message, just to dig that knife in a little deeper.

"Rue?" McKenzie asked, touching my shoulder. "You okay?"

She tried to look at my phone screen, but I flinched and turned it away. "I'm fine," I said. Or I meant to say. It came out more like a gurgled whisper. Launching from the couch, I hurried by the food spread with my head down and took the stairs to the main floor two at a time. My legs, sore from derby practice, screamed at me as I went.

I knew this would happen. I *knew* this would happen, but I did it anyway. Because I was stupid. Because I didn't learn. Because past Samantha wanted to take her revenge on me for letting myself get fooled twice. Shame on me—wasn't that how the saying went?

Shame on me.

Who cares, I told myself. *We dated for, like, a week. He's a prick. A fake. A cookie cutter.*

A lot of other choice words.

The insults were cheap tape on my insides, and the stickiness wasn't holding. I felt something crack, something else shatter. My skin heated with my fury—fury that I was so broken up over *Landry Harrison.* That I was so emotional. But I couldn't reason my way out of it. No amount of logic or anger could tame me.

By the time I reached the front door, ignoring a hello from Rhonda's spouse, stupid, ugly tears were rolling down my face. I wiped at them, practically slapping myself as I did. *Stupid, stupid, stupid.* Pulled a muscle wrenching open my car door. Ripped out my phone.

Reread that same stupid message.

Are you ducking kidding me right now?

Stupid autocorrect. I hit the call button, insisting he talk to me like a man, even if I'd sound like a toad. Even if he lost his balls along with his phone.

It went straight to voicemail.

You're a piece of work, I texted instead, then chucked

my phone onto the passenger seat. He wasn't worth my time. And now LARP party-day was ruined.

I sobbed, then screamed at the fact that I was sobbing, as I reversed out of the driveway. I had to leave. There was little I loathed more than crying in front of people.

Except, maybe, Landry Harrison.

Wyatt called me on my way home. My Nissan announced it on its console screen.

I ignored it.

He called one more time as I pulled into my driveway, but I wasn't in the mood to talk to anyone. I was shocked my window didn't shatter when I slammed the car door and marched into my house, locking knob and dead bolt behind me as if it could somehow shut out the storm following me, growing ever stronger.

I fled to the bathroom. Sure enough, I had lines of mascara streaking down my face. Great. I'd worn makeup every stupid day this week because I'd wanted to impress a *salesman*. And boy, did he sell. Gold star for you, Landry. You cracked me. Congratulations.

I splashed my face with cold water before getting way too much soap to scrub it. I scrubbed until it burned. Dried it none too gently. I had too much energy. I could have run a triathlon right then. And yet all I wanted to do was crawl under my covers for the next year and tell my therapist to up my dosage.

Bed won over energy. I closed the blinds, shut my door, and huddled in the darkness, only the thinnest, gutsiest tendrils of sunlight peeking through the slats. Burying my face into my pillow, I considered taking some nighttime cold medicine so I could just . . . turn off for a while.

Stupid, stupid, stupid.

And, like a stupid person, I pulled my phone out again.

He hadn't responded to my texts. Coward. He always had been. If I didn't know where he lived, I bet he would have just not showed up. Ghosted me all over again. Did men ever grow up?

I scrolled back up. It didn't make sense. Some stupid, hopeful, stupid part of me thought it didn't make sense. Surely I had misread his meaning . . . all twenty times I'd reread the message. Surely something was amiss.

FRIDAY • 4:45 PM

Landry: You have dinner plans yet?

Me: Depends if you're offering or if I'm cooking

Landry: 🦦 Nah I'm bying. Eat in or out?

Me: Iiiiinnnnnn
Wait, we'll already be out. Out?
You're the best

Landry: I try

SATURDAY • 7:07 AM

Landry: I'm going to go in as soon as they open at nine. Meet you their?

Me: Yep. Rhonda's addy is on the FB page. Call me on your shiny new brick if you get lost!

SATURDAY • 12:14 PM

Me: New phone yet?

Landry: Listen, I've been thinking. Please don't take offense to this. LARP and all this nerd stuff isn't really for me. It's a big part of who you are. It IS who you are. I just think . . . it's been fun, but maybe it's better that we go our separate ways.

Me: Are you ducking kidding me right now? You're a piece of work.

I blinked at the screen, my eyes dried out, the bright blue light not helping. I felt like I'd spent the last hour puking. Nope, only one way to interpret *that*.

I set my phone down and rubbed my eyes, forcing myself to take deep breaths. But then my brain folded over, my hands stopped, and I sat upright. Grabbed my phone again. Scrolled up, then down, through the messages.

Since when had Landry learned to spell?

He never capitalized LARP, despite it being an acronym. There were a couple other words I would have expected to be misspelled, or at least have typos.

I hit the phone icon atop the screen to call him. Straight to voicemail again.

Maybe I was going to be one of "those" people, the desperate ones who couldn't take no for an answer, the ones producers *loved* casting for reality shows, but this was weird, and if nothing else, I deserved to be shattered in person, damn it.

"Fine," I snapped, throwing my covers off and retrieving my car keys. I was going to his apartment. Either to talk it out or to egg his place, I hadn't decided.

I was nearly out the door when my phone buzzed, lodging my heart in my chest, but it was only Wyatt again.

Fearing Mom had fallen down the stairs or something, I answered. "What?"

"Rue?"

My larynx froze. That wasn't Wyatt's voice. It was Landry's.

"Hey," he went on, "I am *so* sorry, but I'm not going to make it. My car is being super weird." He sighed. "It won't start, and the screen won't turn on. I've been troubleshooting it all morning."

I swallowed, leaning against my front door. Cleared my thick throat. "Y-Your car broke down?"

"Yeah, sorry. Wyatt's a little closer, and I didn't want to ruin your party."

In the background, my brother yelled, "HEY."

I cleared my throat again. Turned away from the door, then back to it.

"Rue?"

"Do you have your new phone?" I said over him, trying to keep my voice steady.

"No . . . that's why I'm using Wyatt's. I haven't been able to go in yet."

My lips parted. Leaning against the door, I sank to the floor.

"Rue, are you okay?"

"Landry," I said measured, not wanting emotion to leak into my voice. "Were you texting me this afternoon?"

"No . . . my laptop is inside. Are you okay?"

I laughed. It felt like a hair ball coming up my throat—or what I imagined a dry hair ball ripping up my esophagus would feel like. "Landry, I got a text from you two hours ago. You broke up with me."

A pause. "*What?*"

Putting the phone on speaker, I opened up my messages and read the text to him.

"Rue"—I heard some wind and wondered if he'd walked outside, or at least out of the apartment complex's garage—"I didn't send that. Was it from my number? Who the hell sent that?"

"Yeah, from your number. And I don't know." I laughed again, a little less painful this time. Definitely was not going to share the emotional turmoil I had over a fake text. Embarrassment and relief coiled together, stretching me out from the inside, sucking away my strength. "I was about to come find you, because the texter used perfect grammar." *And to tell you off,* I didn't share.

A dry, unmirthful laugh came through. "Well, then." Another sigh. "Do you think you could track the GPS?"

I hurried to my laptop. "I can." I checked the history and pulled up the web page he'd used. "But when I called, it went to voicemail."

"If it was on, it should have something."

"What's wrong with your car?" I asked as the page loaded. "Do Teslas break down?"

"Not really . . . they don't have an engine. It's something electrical, but it's . . . weird. Like, I don't know. Like someone janked it up on purpose. I don't know how this much damage could happen on accident."

The page loaded, and I zoomed in on the address. My hand stilled over the track pad.

"Rue?"

"Rhonda's house," I said. "Landry, the last known location is Rhonda's house."

"The party?"

"Yeah, the party." I swallowed, and my pulse picked up. Why would Landry's phone be at Rhonda's house?

"Maybe she did pick it up," he began, skeptical. We'd already asked Rhonda and the others at Herospect if they'd seen it.

"But then who is texting from it?" I finished.

My guts plummeted to my ankles as my mind spun things together like a hungry spider. Nail in my tire. Phone lost at LARP. Text from Rhonda's house. Cameron taking my purse. Cameron at the park. Cameron refusing to give Landry a ride.

Cameron excusing himself to the bathroom right before I got this text.

I swore.

"What? What's happening?" Landry asked.

"I think Cameron might have your phone." Who else would have motivation? McKenzie and I used to be a thing, but both of us had definitely moved on from that, and she was right next to me when the text came in. Cameron hid his contempt for Landry about as well as a cat hid a load of diarrhea. "Oh my gosh. I'm calling the cops."

"Whoa, let's talk through it." A breeze muffled his words. "That might be overeager."

"No," I said, pulling up the number for Lehi police on my computer. "I'm calling the effing cops."

Chapter 16

I DROVE TO Salt Lake City after that, where Landry was having his car towed for repairs. When I got inside, I caught sight of my brother's ginger head and followed it back into a little lounge area for customers, where Landry was nursing what I suspected to be a Coke Zero.

"Hey," I said, and Landry throttled into alertness and set the cup down. "Do they know what's going on yet—"

And suddenly Landry was there, all man-wall in front of me, his arms wrapped just below torniquet strength around my shoulders. "I am so sorry," he murmured into my hair.

I hugged him back, as much as I could with my arms half pinned. "For what?"

He pulled back and looked me over. "For fake breaking up with you."

I rolled my eyes. "It wasn't you."

"Still."

I flushed. I'd checked the mirror before I left my house— applied some concealer just to be sure. I wasn't red. No sign of crying, except for looking a little tired, which hopefully the white eyeliner adjusted for. There wasn't any evidence of my afternoon roller coaster.

Or maybe, yet again, Landry knew me better than I gave him credit for.

Relaxing, I smiled. "It's okay. Car?"

"They don't know yet, but it looks like sabotage." He grimaced. "The malfunction isn't normal. The mechanic is looking into it."

"Okay." I nodded, and he dropped his arms. "We want a full report when they figure it out so I can hand it over to the police."

Wyatt, on the couch, blurted, "You actually called them?"

He seemed more or less caught up on the situation. "Uh, yes? Because theft and vehicle sabotage are illegal? And maybe stalking?"

Otherwise, how did Cameron know where Landry lived? A shudder coursed up my spine as I thought, *Maybe that was why he was so preoccupied with giving Landry a ride home yesterday.*

Had he followed us in the interim? Followed Landry?

"Maybe it's not him," Landry offered, sensing my train of thought.

"Name another possible suspect and I'll agree with you," I protested.

Landry opened his sexy Cupid's-bow mouth, but no sound came out of it. Instead, he ran a hand back through his hair. "Yeah, I don't know. I'm just glad you didn't believe that text."

I schooled my features. "Good thing you're a bad speller."

He grinned. "My best feature."

"You know . . ." My brother walked up, swirling two coffee stirrers inside an empty foam cup. "This"—he gestured between us with his free hand—"doesn't really add up. I feel like I'm on *Punk'd* or something."

"Rude, Wyatt." I leaned into Landry and slid my hand into his back pocket. "Maybe try not stereotyping for once."

He had the decency not to point out my hypocrisy on the subject.

Yes, the Tesla was sabotaged. Someone had used a hammer drill to get through the chassis, then pulled wires. I faxed in the dealership report, then turned in a paper copy to the police station myself.

I knew police work was slow, but to my surprise, I got a call later that week. The detective on the case said it was an open-and-shut case. While Drakon was a brave and noble ranger in-game, in real life, he was as cowardly as they come. It didn't take long for the officers to poke a hole in his story, and the moment they did, he confessed to everything and pled for leniency. Didn't even wait for a plea bargain. The tire damage was a misdemeanor, but the work he did to Landry's Tesla was a felony.

Which was how Landry and I ended up at the local precinct to write down and record our testimonials. For whatever reason, the officer overseeing mine made me do it twice. I was a lot more colorful the second time around.

While Landry was still writing, I approached the receptionist. "Is Cameron Chussey being held here?" I wasn't exactly sure how criminal processing worked, but I knew it was too early for him to have gone to trial.

"He is," he replied after a moment.

My gut burned like I'd eaten too-hot soup. "Can I talk to him?"

The guy behind the desk paused, rolled his lips together, and picked up the phone. "Hold on." He typed in a three-digit extension and stuck the phone on his shoulder. "Hey, Mark? One of the witnesses is asking to see Cameron Chussey. Yeah . . . uh-huh. Sure."

He hung up. "Just a minute."

I hung out by the desk so I wouldn't be forgotten. Checked the hallway for Landry, but he wasn't done yet. Glanced at my Google News feed. A few minutes later, a policeman in his forties stepped out, a file under his arm.

"Samantha Thompson?"

"That's me." I stuck my phone in my pocket.

He didn't look happy, but he said, "Five minutes, and I'm going to stay back there with you."

I nodded. "Thanks."

He gestured for me to follow him, and he led me down a different hallway than where I'd gone to testify. Sure enough, just like in the movies, there were holding cells in the back. Only two, and one was empty. Cameron sat on the bench in the closest one, wearing a Beastie Boys T-shirt with a plaid button-up over it. His hair looked mussed, and he had dark circles under his eyes, like he hadn't slept well. Unsurprising.

He glanced up at our approach and leapt to his feet. "Rue!" he exclaimed. "I wanted to—"

"What the hell is wrong with you?" I shouted, and as if my

voice were a physical force, he took a step back. "Why would you *ever* do something like that? What is your problem?"

He paled. "It's not what it sounds like—"

"So your confession was just make-believe." My voice was low, deadpan. I stepped closer to the bars, but Officer Mark put out his hand, insisting I stay back. So I planted my heels instead. "I don't like you, Cameron. Not like that. And now, not at all. This is what creepy people do." I jutted my finger toward the bars. "This is what *sociopaths* do."

His jaw tensed. "I'm not a sociopath."

"Then why are you acting like one?" I flung my arms up, almost hitting Mark. "Was that even your sister at the park? My brother's birthday party? Or did you follow me there like you followed Landry to his apartment?"

Cameron said nothing. After a beat, his gaze dropped to the floor. That heat in my gut shifted ice cold. Part of me wished I hadn't asked so I could be happy in my ignorance. But I also knew from experience that avoiding something because it was uncomfortable never turned out well in the end.

"I'm going to get a restraining order."

His eyes shot back up. "What? That's not fair."

I inched toward the bars again. "Tell me *one thing* that isn't fair about that. Even without it, there's no way in hell Rhonda's letting you play again. I hope you can turn this around and live a half-normal life. I really hope you do. But I will *not* be in it." I had no idea what Cameron's sentencing would be. I'd talked it out with Landry multiple times before this. He could get up to a few months in jail (according to Google, anyway) and a steep fine, plus community service. I wanted to push for the maximum punishment, but Landry had a much softer heart than I did.

Cameron's expression was something between supremely pissed and utterly devastated. Turning to Mark, I said, "I'm done."

He made no comment on the exchange, just tilted his head toward the hallway and had me follow him back to the reception area. He kept going—back to his desk, I assume—and I spotted Landry near the desk, on his phone. Sounded like a work call, so I hovered by him, waiting for him to finish.

He ended it quickly. "Hey, what happened?"

I shrugged. "I'll tell you about it on the way home." To the receptionist, I said, "Thanks."

He nodded without looking up. Snatching Landry's hand, I entwined our fingers and pulled him through the storm doors and into the parking lot. I was ready to be done with this.

We were nearly to the car when an urge overtook me. Dropping Landry's hand, I stepped in from of him, grabbed the collar of his polo, and jerked his face down to mine. Pressed my lips hard to his. Tilted my head and layered them.

His hands pressed into my hips as he kissed me back. After a moment, he pulled away. "What's that for?"

I kept my grip on his collar. "Thank you for being normal." I drew in a deep breath. Let it out. "Thank you for being nice. Thank you for listening." I placed a soft peck on his mouth. "And thank you . . . for coming back."

He smiled that perfect smile, which I still thought was stupid but absolutely loved. Squeezing my sides, he said, "You're very welcome."

"And"—I released him, but stayed close—"thank you for not breaking up with me."

He laughed. "I will never break up with you."

Raising an eyebrow, I countered, "Never say never."

He shrugged. "Maybe I like punishment. Kidding, kidding."

"Maybe I'll make you sign your name to it." I smoothed his rumpled collar. "Maybe. I might be tired of you by next week." (That was a lie.)

"Better step up my game, then."

Speaking of games . . .

"You approach the mouth of the cave," Rhonda explained, standing outside that copse of trees where I'd once harassed my very awesome and attentive boyfriend. "Water sprays up against the sides, and there's a gust of heat from the mouth. As you move closer, you see that the cavern doesn't extend out, into the sea, but down."

"I test for traps." Adelaide, our new rogue, inched forward.

"You can't sense any from here," Rhonda said.

I pulled my foam sword and shook red hair out of my face. Deep ruby red to match Lukartha, my new dragon-ilk character. As a fighter, I was ready to head in first. "I grab a stone and toss it." I mimed the gesture.

The group was silent. Gooseflesh raised on my arms. In the theater of my mind, I could see it all—the black rock misted with sea water, the overcast sky, the pit before us.

After several breaths, Rhonda said, "You don't hear it land."

"I've got some rope," I offered. "I'll go first."

The others nodded. Turning to the cleric dressed in white and blue, I asked, "You sure you're a healer?"

It was game one, so we were all low level, and Lukartha and Judge didn't have any backstory together.

Landry/Judge nodded. "I've got your back."

Breaking character, I grinned at him before heading into the trees, feeling far more confident than a level-one fighter should.

Because from now on, we would fight all of our monsters together.

THE END

Acknowledgments

Thank you to everyone who helped me with this book! My first thanks goes to my husband, Jordan, for always giving me the time and support I need to write. LOVE YOU.

Next, many thanks to Kingdoms, a local LARPing group, for letting me slink around their event and pester people with questions. Thank you especially to Jessica Childers, Weston Childers, Alyssa Tsuchiya, Whitney Hanks, Jason Rogers, Aimee Moore, and Andrew Moore.

Many thanks to those who beta read for me, including Leah O'Neill, Whitney Hanks (again—this is her third mention in this book), Bill Giles, Lisa Book, Brekke Felt, Cathy Webb, and Amy Lauderback. Also, thank you to Allen Sangster for helping me with legal stuffs.

Huge thank you to Kristy S. Gilbert, because I literally would not even try to publish these if she weren't taking the reins and steering the carriage. I also want to thank my proofreader, Jennie Stevens, and cover designer, Michelle Argyle.

Thank you to my agent, Marlene Stringer, for dealing with the audio rights for this series. That's right, folks, you can LISTEN to this book too!

And, always and forever, many thanks to my Father in Heaven for my brain and my abilities. I owe you one (million).

Charlie N. Holmberg is a Wall Street Journal and Amazon Charts bestselling author of fantasy and romance fiction, and writes contemporary romance under C. N. Holmberg. She is published in over 20 languages, has been a finalist for a RITA award and multiple Whitney awards, and won the 2020 Whitney for Novel of the Year for Adult Fiction. Born in Salt Lake City, Charlie was raised a Trekkie alongside three sisters who also have boy names. She is a BYU alumna, plays the ukulele, and owns too many pairs of glasses. She currently lives with her family in Utah.

Visit her at www.charlienholmberg.com.